Werewolf Tale II

As Shane looked up, and then in his direction, his sudden stop, and the shifting of his expression from blank to surprised, made holding back the many kinds of expressions Alex felt ready to display difficult. At least until, after a few seconds, Shane glanced at the minivan, and then made a beeline for him.

Despite the setting and time of day, some level of concern filled Alex's head as he approached. "Are you happy now?" Shane asked once he was close enough for his lowered voice to still carry a frustrated, possibly confrontational, tone.

Alex forced himself to speak, to not let Shane dominate things. "Not a hundred percent."

Shane huffed out his nose and shook his head.

With a month and a half passed from the day he was bitten, Alex Stryker's second full moon approaches.

Though now better versed in what he must do, Shane remains a wild card in his life. Along with the growing risk of a dangerous hunt, and loss of sources of animal prey.

Werewolf Tale II

Author – Adam Gulledge

Cover Artist – Natalya Gosteva

Editor – Sean Gerace

- Renegade Publications -
2019

First Printing: 2019

ISBN: 978-1-7325210-5-6

www.werewolftale.info

Contents

Acknowledgements

My cover artist, Natalya Gosteva. She was a pleasure to work with, and her style continues to impress.

My editor, Sean Gerace. Once again, his input was invaluable in shaping the final draft of this novel.

The readers and buyers of the original Werewolf Tale, and the fans who have followed Alex's story for all these years. It's been all kinds of fun reading your feedback and speaking with all of you.

Chapter 1 - Father and Son

Friday, October 7th, 2011 – Sugar Land, Texas
Moon Phase - Waxing Gibbous
Days until the Full Moon - 5

Alex Stryker sighed into his helmet as he continued to watch his father direct and assist the other police officers. Several minutes had passed since they'd reunited, and judging by the returning canine units, the search of the area was wrapping up. With the breezes still going west, Alex kept a close eye on them in case they turned their attention towards him.

After a minute, his concerns about them relaxed, allowing the image of Shane's snarl-twisted muzzle to return to his thoughts. Twinges of the fear he'd felt towards the end of the encounter with him came with it, and before he could brush them aside, he noticed his father glance back at him. A thumbing towards him followed, and once the two officers nodded, the distance between them began to close.

"I need to get back to overseeing things, so I can't talk for long," he said once he was close. Alex nodded. "They didn't find him though, so just tell me what happened between you two. We'll talk more at home if need be."

Alex took a breath and exhaled to relieve what pressure remained in his chest. He'd seen few hints of Shane until very recently. He had to be lying about the last claim he made.

"When I found him, I tried to get him to leave, but he just scoffed at the idea. Then I started questioning him, about why he bit me, his reasoning for it."

"Was that why you were upset before?" his father asked after a second.

Alex nodded. "I didn't realize until a few hours ago how flawed his reasoning was."

"I see," his father replied with a quieter voice. It went back to its normal pitch before he continued. "What was his reasoning?"

"Remember that girl Nathan and I tried to help?" Alex's father nodded. "He told me she was a werewolf too, and because she got her blood on me when I was helping her, he thought I was already infected."

The expression on his father's face flipped between concern and suspicion as he spoke, before settling on something similar to what Nathan had displayed before. "That makes no sense to me," he eventually replied, "but keep that in mind until tonight. Did anything else happen?"

"Yeah. I asked him if he'd even considered leaving me alone in case he was wrong about that. He wasn't having any of it, and started taking things personally."

"How personally?"

Alex sighed quietly. "Enough to start snarling and staring me down."

His father hummed. "You weren't confrontational in any way?"

Alex stalled and looked down. "I was angry. Who wouldn't be?"

"I know, Son, but that was why I was more worried about you than him." After a moment of silence, Alex's father continued. "You didn't change, though. That's most important."

"I guess."

"Anything else?"

Alex shook his head, despite what had followed his own emotional statements during the encounter. "He took off when the canines came close. Said he'd defend himself if they found him, but if they didn't..."

"By this point, they won't. The animals are what we're after."

"That's good."

"Which way did he go, though?"

Alex glanced to his right for a second. "North, I think."

"Toward the warehouse and office buildings?"

"Yeah, but there's a creek that way too." His father's gaze inched to his left. "Who knows where he went after that."

"I'll venture a few guesses, if he's stuck like that."

Alex then imagined Shane hiding under the bridge to the west. The basin was well-concealed, and he could easily hide there until the sun went down.

As another potential spot came to mind, his father continued. "I don't want you going looking for him, though."

"Even to---"

"No, Son. I said don't push your luck before, and you almost did. The last thing we need right now is you changing in broad daylight."

Alex's drive to argue died when he glanced past his father's shoulder, at the officers and canine units. He sighed quietly. "I know."

"If you're still angry, then do me a favor: go home and relax. I'll be finished here soon."

"Alright," Alex soon said, to which his father patted his shoulder. "I'll see you later then, Dad."

"You too, Son."

Alex waited for his father to turn around and walk away before starting his motorcycle's engine. Once he'd turned around himself, he drove toward the street where his father had "pulled him over", slowing down and stopping as the bridge he'd imagined Shane hiding under came into view.

There was no sign of him, and the currently west-bound breezes were of no help.

Chapter 2 - A Respite

Friday, October 7th, 2011
Moon Phase - Waxing Gibbous
Days until the Full Moon - 5

Where Shane had gone was next on Alex's mind. It wasn't long before he was picturing the wooded lot near his house, with Shane's still-snarling face peeking from behind one of the trees. The image made him draw a sigh yet kept him and his motorcycle still for a while after.

Once he'd resumed driving, Alex continued straight ahead instead of taking the right turn that would lead him toward his neighborhood. After a few minutes, he was in the parking lot of his workplace and making his way inside.

Daniel was quick to greet him after setting down the trade in his hands. "Hey, man."

Alex gave him a brief glance before replying. "Hey, Daniel."

"You change your mind about the RPG session?"

Alex shook his head. "Just wanted to hang out for a while."

"Fair enough." As Daniel went back to reading, Alex headed for the single-issues section and flipped through the stock until he found one that looked pleasing.

He was several pages in before his mind started to drift, back to the encounter with Shane. Back to the scent of blood on his breath, his vicious snarling, and the things he claimed he would do. As the memories put pressure on Alex's throat, he did his best to not look like something was bothering him, despite the lack of nearby bodies.

A while later, the sounds of dice rolling began to travel from the back of the shop and Alex turned his head towards the source. *Some gaming would be fun right about now...* After replacing the comic, a look outside revealed a nearly set sun--half-an-hour, at best, was what remained of the evening. No one had called him or sent any texts, but his father had to be done with work by now.

What Alex found in the gaming room was his boss acting once again as the dungeon master, and three players. Fresh tension grew in his chest as their attention focused on him, and as he remained silent.

"Hey, Alex." Trevor said.

Alex returned half of his boss' greeting.

"We've got a few characters open if you're interested."

Alex instead glanced around the table. "What game is this?"

"GURPS," said one of the older-looking players. "Ever heard of it?"

"Only in relation to the Fallout games," Alex replied.

"That works," Trevor said. "Grab a seat. We'll walk you through the basics."

After a nod to his boss, Alex slipped into the chair closest to the doors. The image of Shane hiding near his house returned as he did so. Going home and potentially finding him there felt less nerve-wracking in comparison; if his father was home, all he'd have to do was say something.

Alex thought better of that idea, and of texting his father, after a few moments. If Shane was serious about his claim, yet hadn't changed back, making him wait made more sense. He would have to give up at some point.

His decision made, Alex refocused on the game and the rules and systems his boss laid out. When the other players chimed in or asked questions, the tension in his chest flared, delaying some of his answers and making him worry that someone would notice, even once the game began in earnest and he was no longer the center of attention.

He wasted little time leaving the store once the game was over and everyone had exchanged pleasantries. Outside, the winds were still blowing west. None of the roads he could take to his house would put him directly east of where Shane could be.

After he reached his neighborhood, Alex altered his route to follow the road running north alongside his house, keeping his attention on the wooded lot as he approached. The sole glance to his side revealed his father's truck in the driveway. When he felt he was close enough, he turned his bike to face the wooded lot and swept the headlight across it. No reflections, nor any moving masses of black or tan, were revealed.

He was less than a full step inside the house before Bailey rushed him, his tail wagging eagerly. Alex didn't bother trying to stop him from jumping to greet him. After the last few hours, his company and attention was too pleasant and welcoming.

Then Bailey noticed something, and his enthusiasm waned. When his muzzle was thrust into the gap between his tee and jacket, Alex let him down and rubbed his head, certain he was noticing and concerned about Shane's fur scent. *I know, boy. I'm okay.*

Saturday, October 8th, 2011
Moon Phase – Waxing Gibbous
Days until the Full Moon – 4

Catching Bailey's scent when he awoke the next morning, Alex rolled over to find his dog was sleeping nearly back to back with him. His dog awoke and lifted his head from the quilt before Alex rubbed his neck. "Good boy."

With another day off work, after what had happened the day before, Alex was hoping one of his friends would be free for the day. Some time with them felt like the best way to spend a few hours.

Once he'd had a shower, he headed to the kitchen. His father was making another pot of coffee while his mother was making breakfast. "Morning, Son."

"Hey, Dad." His reply came out softer than usual.

"You still tired?"

"No. Just thinking about what to do today."

"How did your skating event go yesterday?" his mother asked.

Hearing that, Alex looked towards his father. He didn't make any gestures to the effect of urging him to speak.

"What's wrong?" his mother asked after no answer was given.

Alex's father responded in turn, and what he said was exactly what he didn't want him to. "He didn't take part."

"Why not?"

"Because I told him another animal killing had happened, and then he left and came to the scene."

The confusion on his mother's face held as she turned his attention towards him. "Why would you do that?"

Alex broke eye contact. *Not now.*

"What happened?" His mother's tone now held more worry than before.

Alex pushed the image of Shane holding him down out of his head. His mother didn't need to know that, and his father knew enough already.

"The werewolf that attacked me was there," he eventually said. His mother's expression went horror-stricken upon hearing that, and he couldn't bring himself to say more.

"Alex said he ran away when he heard me and the other officers coming," his father said after a moment, to which his mother placed a hand over her heart, and he placed one on her shoulder. Only the skillet and coffeemaker made any noise for a while after.

When the further questioning Alex was anticipating never came—his guess was because he and his father had come home safe—he made his way to the fridge. When he was close to his mother, he swore he could feel the tension and concern radiating from her. The presence of her fear scent only helped the impression.

He was finishing pouring a glass of milk when she spoke up again. "No one saw anything?"

"No," his father said. "The officers would've radioed me otherwise."

"So, that's it?"

Alex could tell the question was directed at him; despite the innocence of it, he was reminded of Shane's threat. "Until I run into him again," he eventually said.

"You didn't have to run into him last time, Son." his father replied.

"No, but I told you he's been showing up where my friends and I work. I can't control that."

"Regardless, Alex, don't go putting yourself at risk."

Alex looked away and sighed, eventually answering with, "I'll try." Promising anything in relation to Shane would feel hollow, given how free he was to do as he pleased.

When the following silence held for another long period, he set his glass aside and offered his mother a hug. Her fear scent was still present, leaving him hoping it would dissipate before breakfast was over.

Chapter 3 ⁃ There's Something...

Saturday, October 8th, 2011
Moon Phase – Waxing Gibbous
Days until the Full Moon – 4

As that time neared, it became more obvious that Bailey was waiting for something. "I know, boy," Alex said as he walked past him, toward the kitchen. He made for his pet's leash once his plate was in the sink, which drew excited wagging and panting from Bailey.

Outside, the morning fog was thinning out, though enough remained to obscure part of the lot across the street. Alex focused on it for a bit before leading Bailey toward it.

He heard no footsteps outside of his own as he drew closer, but eventually a pungent scent slowed him down. Bailey noticed it too, only to shy away from the source--a single tree--once he found it.

By then, Alex's distaste for the scent had taken on a worrying edge. The scent was new, but once Shane's threat flashed back to mind, he could see no other explanation for the feelings. He had been here, either last night or within the last eight hours.

Though unsure of which, Alex soon felt an urge to cover up Shane's scent with his own, even if all it signaled to him was he'd noticed it. He spent a few minutes counting the frequency of passing cars, and only when he was certain he wouldn't be spotted did he make his move.

Back at home, Alex kept the discovery to himself, and spent the time until he left the house again reading in his room. Bailey spent much of that time resting near his legs, much to his appreciation.

Alex's first stops were at Blue Moon and Half-Price Books. Neither had any hints of Shane's scent, which left Nathan's place of work. When he arrived, he found his sedan parked near the entrance, but no sign of him inside. Just a new employee and a pair of customers.

"Welcome to Gamestop," the employee said as Alex walked in. "Looking for anything?"

"No, just coming in for a bit," Alex replied. The employee--Josh by his name badge--nodded. "Is Nathan here, or did he go on break?"

"Yeah. He's on break."

Alex nodded this time. "I'll look around until he comes back, then." A moment later he began his walk of the store, trying to avoid where the other customers had been. He didn't find Shane's scent. An all-clear once again.

When Nathan returned, he lifted his lunch's styrofoam cup to serve as a wave. "Hey, man. What's going on?"

"Not much. Just figured I'd stop by."

Once his friend had clocked back in, Josh asked for his break. "Sure. We're not gonna be busy until later." The two customers left shortly after Josh did. "Checking for what's-his-face again?" Nathan asked.

Alex nodded. "No hint of him, so we're good."

"I didn't see him either, but thanks for confirming it."

"No problem." Alex continued after a moment. "I don't think he's spending every waking moment just watching us, but..." Alex couldn't find the words to complete his sentence for a time. "I don't know. He could be."

"You have run into him a lot lately."

"Yeah."

"You sound a bit down," Nathan said after a bit. "Something happen?"

Alex looked behind himself. "Yesterday, yeah."

"Let me guess. He showed up at the skatepark?"

"No," Alex replied with a shake of his head. "I skipped the event."

"What for?"

"Dad was supposed to be there, but he got a call at the last minute."

"Ouch. Still though, why didn't you take part? He could've come later."

"Yeah, he could've..."

Alex paused long enough to tip Nathan off that that wasn't the whole story. "Did he get called to another animal killing?"

"Yeah, he did."

"Aw, geez." Nathan's voice then lowered, as if someone could emerge from the storage room at any minute. "What happened?"

"Shane was there."

Nathan looked over to the door, then back at his friend. "Human or..."

"Werewolf."

"Oh, shit."

Alex looked behind himself again. "Yeah. No one saw him though, I think."

"Can't imagine what would've happened if they did."

"Me either," Alex said, his thoughts refilling with his fears of being exposed. "And when I found him, he just scoffed off my suggestion to shift back."

"That's not good."

"No kidding, but when the police started coming close, he bolted and told me to as well."

"Really? Huh." Nathan's expression began to show a bit of relief.

"He talks a big game, but he still has some common sense."

"At least. Was that all he did?"

"No." Alex took a quiet breath. "He and I got to talking after I found him." He expected Nathan to remark on that, but when he didn't, Alex continued. "If I'd known how he was going to react, I would've left."

"Why? What happened?"

Alex exhaled, trying not to allow his bubbling emotions to surface. "I told him what you said about the bite, asked why he didn't wait and see. Then he got angry, started snarling, got in my face and got me to cower." Nathan then exhaled noticeably, and in a prolonged way. "I didn't say your name."

"OK. Scared me for a minute."

"Sorry." Alex took a deep breath before continuing. "I tried not to let him get to me, but then I found out what Marcus told me is truer than I thought."

"What was that?"

"That I seem to shy away from this guy when he acts threatening."

"Can't blame you. I'd be worried about someone like that too."

"No. Not just that." Alex said. "I mean shying away from him like a submissive animal would."

Nathan looked away as if to consider what he was told. "I don't know, man. That sounds like a stretch."

"It's not. I felt like I had to curl up and look weaker to make him stop threatening me." Alex licked his lips and sighed.

"Did it?"

"No, it didn't." The quivering in Alex's breathing was becoming more noticeable. "And it made me sick. Him holding me down and threatening to maul me."

Nathan didn't speak for a minute, and made only small movements while leaning against the counter. "At least he didn't hurt you."

"He would've." Alex's next inhale was wracked with trembles. "He snapped his jaws behind my neck, and then kept them by my ear..."

Nathan glanced at the door again before saying, "Calm down, man. Take it easy."

Alex dropped the rest of his reply at that. He could feel his blood pumping in his ears by then, and how fast his pulse had become. As he then worked to correct his shaky breaths, he kept his back to the store's entrance, and his eyes off his friend.

When he heard the door open a minute later, Alex pivoted to keep the customer from seeing his face and pretended to browse the cases on the nearby wall. One sniffle escaped him as he waited for the store to empty, though he quickly faked it as a running nose, to which Nathan passed him a paper towel.

Once the customer was gone, he and Nathan continued. "You alright?" Nathan asked.

"Yeah," Alex said before circling the counter and tossing the paper towel. "Anyway, aside from that, when do you get off work?"

"About two hours. Why? Did you have something in mind?"

"Yeah. I was curious if you were interested in hanging out for a while."

"Sure. Where at?"

"My place."

"That works. I'll let you know when I'm on my way."

Chapter 4 – ...I Think You Should Know

Saturday, October 8th, 2011
Moon Phase – Waxing Gibbous
Days until the Full Moon – 4

After a nod to his friend, Alex left the store. The drive home gave him more time to relax, but within an hour, something began to bug him. What had mentioning the incident accomplished? He'd no doubt made his friend more curious, and despite what Shane had threatened, he didn't want to freak him, much less Catherine or Marcus, out more if he could help it. Even if the only things that truly seemed to disturb them were him shifting and the sight of his werewolf form.

Once Nathan arrived and had a glass of water in his hands, the two of them got to talking, and eventually decided on some gaming. Bailey stayed near Nathan initially, earning several pets and belly rubs for his choice.

"Hey, question," Nathan said as they reached a new level. "You have your schedule worked out for when the full moon comes?"

"Yeah," Alex said after pausing the game. "I've got that day off work, and the one before, and I'm skipping my classes too."

"Probably for the best."

"Yeah. I'd rather not take any risks and be around anyone."

They completed another level before Nathan spoke up again. "Actually, I've been meaning to ask..."

Alex paused the game.

"Is this guy trying to drag you into what he's doing?"

Alex glanced aside, confused as to what that meant.

"These animal killings," Nathan clarified. "Is he trying to get you involved?"

His friend had yet to finish speaking before Alex felt a jolt through his nerves. His thoughts immediately centered on Marcus, the only one of his friends that, up to now, had raised any suspicion about the animal deaths.

As the seconds got away from him, Alex could feel his stomach close up. "No," he replied with a shake of his head.

"That's good to hear, but you don't have a choice otherwise, do you?"

The feeling of a closing stomach intensified to a torso-wide organ punch. *Damn it. When...shit.* As shakiness leeched into his breathing, Alex couldn't stop thinking about when Nathan had figured things out, and how. About what had gone through Catherine and Marcus's heads if they had been informed.

"It's okay, man. I understand, and I don't blame you." Nathan said after a time.

Alex only exhaled in reply.

As if sensing the drop in his mood, Bailey got up and moved closer, settling back down near his legs. Alex wasted no time petting him, his warm fur and curious stare giving him something else to focus on. As he did so, he tried to draw some morale from how calm his friend was, how patient he was being. He had to have figured things out the night he shifted in front of everyone. It was the only date that made sense.

"Thanks," Alex eventually said.

"No problem." Another stretch of silence went by. "Was that something you had to figure out?"

Alex nodded.

His friend sighed. "And that was why you snuck out that night, right?"

Alex took a breath. "Yeah."

"I thought so. Made any plans for next time?"

Alex hesitated. "No."

Nathan didn't reply.

"I mean I know my options; I just don't have anything set."

"Trying not to think about it too much?"

"Yeah, or what I have to do."

"Can't blame you."

Alex exhaled and things went quiet again.

"So you know," Nathan said after a while, "I brought this up with Catherine and Marcus too."

Alex felt his chest tensing up again at that, his throat seeming to take some of it as well.

"It did scare them a little when I told them, and I won't lie, I was nervous too when I realized it."

Alex lightly shook his head after a few seconds. Even though his friend had said he understood, the now-emerging presence of his fear scent was enough of a sign that his fears hadn't faded, and something was drawing them out. Shane's words about his friends trying not to be afraid of him flashed back to mind, as did the mental images of the raccoon, the doe, and his blood-stained paws.

The tension in his chest turned vice-like, and his breathing started to quiver again. All he wanted at that point was to get up and walk away, put some space between him and his friend to allow time to collect himself, or anything to keep from looking upset in front of him again. The thumping of his friend's heart, how much its pace was increasing, enhanced that desire. For all he knew, his friend was more scared of him potentially shifting than anything else and staying nearby was only aggravating that fear.

Yet as much as he felt walking away would help, another part of him couldn't see the move as anything but cowardly. There was nothing he could hide anymore. His friends knew, and that was that. He'd done nothing to hurt them either; the rattled nerves would soon pass.

Those thoughts and assurance went on for a while, helping Alex get his breathing under control and eventually from sounding like he was about to break down. When he spoke again, he followed up what his friend had last said with something he'd remembered. "Not...not seeing any messages from you guys was worrying me."

"Yeah, we did get quiet for a while," Nathan said. "I didn't mean to. I don't think they did either."

Alex took in a lengthy breath and wiped his eyes.

After a bit more silence, Nathan patted his shoulder and asked, "You okay?"

"I guess." His friend gave him some time. "Thanks, for being honest with me."

"You're welcome."

It took several more minutes for Alex's insides to no longer feel stressed, after which he felt as though a boulder had been lifted off his back. Nathan was quick to suggest that they get some food, and before long, the kitchen was smelling of hot, fresh pizza.

As they carried on conversation and ate, in the back of Alex's mind, he wondered how long his friends had known about the eating living things part of his lycanthropy. Marcus had brought the subject up almost two weeks prior, and if Nathan was only now speaking like he'd known, it couldn't have been very many days since they'd figured it out.

Eventually, he pushed the question aside in favor of enjoying his friend's company. It felt more worthwhile anyway.

Chapter 5 - Did He Return?

Sunday, October 9th, 2011
Moon Phase – Waxing Gibbous
Days until the Full Moon – 3

Alex's sleep that night was wracked by nightmares, thanks to the revelations Nathan had dropped as well as his revived fears of what his friends now saw in him. He awoke barely after two-o-clock, his skin drenched in sweat and his heart racing.

Before he moved, Alex could feel Bailey sleeping behind him, as well as the outstretched limb resting atop him. *Thanks, boy. You're the best*, he thought as he reached over and petted him.

* * *

Later that morning, after a shower to truly wake himself up, Alex considered messaging Catherine and Marcus, at least to let them know Nathan had spoken to him. Once he started typing, he took it slow, making sure he worded it exactly as he wanted.

> *Alex S.:* Hey, guys. Nathan mentioned he spoke to you about something that happens to me.
>
> I didn't mean to hide that, but the thought of mentioning it worried me too much. You guys mean a lot to me, and I didn't want to scare you off.

Pausing to read over the message, Alex swore to himself and tried to smile as his eyes watered a bit. After blinking them clear, he read over the message, then decided to add more.

Alex S.: If it helps, that is the last part of this. The rest you already know.

Alex pressed "send" after a few more reads of the text. Bailey nudged his leg shortly after, earning a rubbing of his head and a question that got his tail wagging, "Outside?" After half-an-hour of throwing the ball for his dog, his curiosity about Shane's presence had returned and he urged Bailey to his side. They then crossed the street to the wooded lot, and with a westward breeze blowing by, Alex walked the length of the lot, finding no fresh traces of Shane's scent.

He coaxed Bailey over for some petting once he was satisfied. *Wonder if he's only watching the house now.* Alex couldn't see the point at first, but then started wondering if Shane was sneaking into the backyard. A moment later, he headed towards the road, making a beeline for the backyard; he'd left his blinds open overnight.

Despite that, Alex found no hints of Shane's scent upon the wood that formed the outside windowsill. *Eh. Better check again tonight.*

* * *

"Alex?"

Alex looked up from his dinner when his mother said his name. "Yeah?"

"Are you ready for Wednesday?"

"Um..." Alex glanced at his father, finding his attention on him as well. "Yeah. I should be fine."

"When did you change last time?" his father asked.

"About three-thirty in the afternoon...and that was the day before the full moon, so actually Tuesday afternoon and Wednesday."

"Are you certain that's when it will happen?"

"Pretty certain." His parents didn't reply. "It's all I have to go on, so for all I know, that's when."

"And this lasts for thirty-six hours?" his mother asked.

"Yeah, so around three-thirty Thursday morning, I'll change back." He caught a glance of his mother expressing relief at that.

"You're skipping class on Tuesday then, I hope."

"Yeah, I am." Despite the circumstances, hearing his father advocate for skipping school felt strange. "I'm not taking any risks, and I have those two days off work, so I'm covered."

His father nodded. "Good to know."

Alex dug back into his meal once he was certain the questions had ended. By the time he finished, the sun had completely set and the streetlights were lit. Hoping Shane wasn't nearby, he retrieved Bailey's leash, the clinking of the metal pieces summoning him from his spot by the couch.

Outside, the night sky was dominated by the gibbous moon and the clouds it was illuminating. After cutting himself off from the lights of the house, Alex's nightvision went to work, brightening the things he could see. Eventually, from his position on the porch, his view of the wooded lot was clear.

He saw no hints of large, fuzzy bodies or reflecting eyes, but until he physically went closer, he couldn't be sure. With Bailey growing anxious for a walk, Alex walked him up and down the length of his street, letting him follow and sniff whatever things he found interesting.

As the lot drew closer on the way back, he shielded his eyes from the nearby streetlight until it was behind him. Dozens of crickets were chirping in the grass, with handfuls stopping as he and Bailey made their way to a stretch of turf that ran behind two rows of houses. Alex saw nothing along the north or south lengths, and Shane's scent was once again absent.

Maybe he marked that tree just to unnerve me.

Monday, October 10th, 2011
Moon Phase – Waxing Gibbous
Days until the Full Moon – 2

Alex left for campus early on Monday. It had been a few days since he'd last enjoyed an uninterrupted session of just riding around on his board, and today and tomorrow were the best times to enjoy it before he changed.

As he cruised around behind the main building, his thoughts jumping between the animal hunger and what to do while stuck inside, his brain flashed an image of him skating in his were form. The resulting cringe throughout his muscles slowed him down and got him off the board.

Once in class, he casually took in the scents of the other students. A few of them had new clothes on from the starch scents, and the many scents associated with fast food provoked his stomach. Compared to Friday, the quiet time in class was a nice change of pace, even once the professor entered the room and his worry of having eyes on him came back.

Alex passed on heading to the student lounge after class, opting instead to wait outside the room of his next class. His phone sounded the IM tone a few minutes later as he was growing absorbed in the novel in his hands.

Marcus A.: No harm done, man.

Alex breathed a sigh of relief at the message and replied with his thanks. Though Catherine had yet to reply, he gave her some benefit of the doubt and got back to reading.

Chapter 6 – Familial Plans...

Monday, October 10th, 2011
Moon Phase – Waxing Gibbous
Days until the Full Moon – 2

As soon as class was over and he and Nathan had split up, Alex headed outside and jumped back on his skateboard. The winds had picked up since that morning, sweeping scents from miles upwind into his nostrils and causing his momentum to die when he wasn't following the currents.

After several laps of the main buildings, he headed for his motorcycle and then made his way to the skateshop. The welcoming scents of wax, urethane, and plywood greeted him as the door opened, along with the sounds of several skaters inside the park. Three, he guessed.

At the counters, Walter was looking over and stocking what seemed like new product shipments until he spotted him approaching. "Hey, Alex."

Alex responded in kind.

"Was everything alright the other day?"

"Yeah," Alex said as he slipped his backpack off. "Nothing major."

"Glad to hear it."

Their conversation then trailed into the demo Alex had missed. Although Walter expressed pleasure from how much fun it was, a mention of low overall attendance followed.

"That sucks," Alex said. "Will you still have events, though?"

Walter gave a nod. "Hopefully, we can do one every month so some interest will grow."

"If so, I'm looking forward to the next one."

Once he was inside the park, Alex took note of which spots were being used by the other skaters, mostly the rails and funboxes to his left, before setting his board down and pushing off. He gave himself one lap of the area to watch for any uneasiness--twice he felt twinges of it. The same lap exposed him to several new scents, none that seemed concerning.

In the end, Alex spent much of his first half-hour cruising, only attempting tricks when he felt that the attention of the others wouldn't be on him. His stomach began growling towards the end of the allotted hour, pushing him to leave and get some lunch. The place he chose was brimming with pleasant scents, and he stayed inside long enough to decide to buy a little more food for when the shift was over.

Back at home, with a sniff at the door crack, Alex could just catch Bailey's scent. Within a second of opening the door, he heard his pet's heavy paws impacting the carpet as he ran to greet him. "Good boy," Alex said before Bailey turned his attention to the bag of food in his hand. "Ah, no. Not for you."

Despite his father always sleeping with the door closed, Alex could still hear him snoring as he walked through the living room to the kitchen. In turn, he spent the time until his father awoke reading or throwing handfuls of his role-playing dice across his carpet. When he imagined himself dungeon mastering a game for his friends in his were form, the cringe he'd felt earlier in the day resurfaced, though not as deeply.

When his father did wake, it didn't take long for him to imply he wanted to talk. "I just remembered something I meant to ask you last night."

"What?"

"If you wanted the house to yourself after two or so tomorrow."

Alex replied with little hesitation. "If you and Mom want to do that."

"She has something to do after work tomorrow. It'll just be me here by then."

"Oh, okay. But yeah, sure. That's fine."

"You're putting Bailey out before it happens too, I hope."

"I know. I will." Alex then noticed his pet staring at him, and he rubbed his head. *The first time it was an accident. This one should go smoother.*

Tuesday, October 11th, 2011
Moon Phase – Waxing Gibbous
Time until the Shift - 10 Hours, 51 Minutes

When Alex awoke the next morning, Bailey wasn't sleeping beside him, and the backs of his eyes felt oddly irritated, like something had broken his sleep at its most relaxed moment. After sitting up to look around, he didn't see Bailey on his dog bed either. Seeing 4:39 a.m. on his phone's screen caused little concern, though why he'd woken up so early twice in a row before the full moon remained a mystery.

Forget it. Probably just nerves, Alex thought before he laid his head back down. Though he attempted to get back to sleep, to build up some more energy for what he knew was coming, something kept it from him and he soon sat back up.

After holding off a yawn and wiping his eyes, Alex sat waiting for the irritation behind his eyes to fade. A few breaths through his nose revealed no new scents, though the sight of the guest room's open door gave him an idea where Bailey could be. Once the irritation faded, he slid out of bed, the snoring from his mother providing a good mask for his movement.

He was proven right. Bailey was asleep on the futon in front of the window. He stayed asleep, or so it seemed, until Alex was within a few feet of him, at which point his eyes opened, and his head turned to face his approaching owner.

"Hey, boy," Alex whispered. He got no reaction, but still moved to pet his dog's head. Bailey's head and muzzle moved to follow his hand and arm, leaving Alex wondering what his dog was seeing in him. He then let Bailey sniff him, and while he didn't seem afraid, he didn't seem excited either.

Only once his dog licked him did Alex take the opportunity to pet his head, belly, and back. "You'll be okay, boy." he whispered before standing up and leaving him to his peace.

After getting some water, Alex peered outside from behind the living room curtains. The gibbous moon was uncovered, and its radiance gave everything in sight a slightly silver sheen. He closed them again upon noticing headlights steadily illuminating the road across from him and then returned to his room.

His father began to stir over an hour later, by which time Alex was absorbed in his comic collection and imagining what Nathan's next RPG session would involve. Within the silence of his room, he could hear every shuffle, groan, and footstep, even the sound of a kiss, and waited for his father to leave his bedroom.

When he did, looking as though he was still waking up, Alex gave him a wave as soon as his attention was on him.

"You're up early," his father said in reply after a curious-sounding, muffled hum.

Alex shrugged. "Couldn't get back to sleep."

"Is everything okay?"

"Yeah. Nothing's wrong."

His father didn't immediately reply. "Alright. Morning then, Son."

Alex replied in kind, then slipped into the bathroom for a shower. By the time he reentered the kitchen, numerous coffee grind scents were dominating the space, but were easily pushed aside by the scents of the leftovers he warmed up.

He was halfway through his meal when his mother came into view, looking freshly awoken herself and glad to see him. After getting a cup of coffee for herself, she floated a question aimed at him. "You didn't hurt yourself last time, did you?"

Alex pushed the resurfacing memory of breaking his metatarsals aside. "No, I was fine."

"Then you'll be okay without us around?"

Even though he was certain his mother knew the answer, Alex cracked a small smile and answered as calmly as he could. "Yeah. I'll be fine."

"What about afterwards?"

Alex reached for and held his bullet and necklace at that. "I'll be hungry after it's done, but that's it."

"Not for animals, I hope," his father replied.

"No. Normal food works."

"Then what about when you will be hungry for them?"

Alex stalled. After several seconds, his father said his name in a questioning tone. He quietly sighed once before answering. "I know. I don't know when it'll happen, but I'll be careful."

His answer drew a concerned breath from his mother, pulling his attention to her. Her expression was telling of what she was feeling, so Alex got up from his chair, stepped closer to her, and wrapped his arms around her. Her fear scent was already leaking from her skin.

"I know what to do this time, but if I can't help it, I can't help it." His mother didn't respond; he swore he heard a quiver in her breaths.

"It would be nice to know if you could avoid that." The pitch in his father's voice was an obvious giveaway; he'd already put the same pieces together. One screw up and he would be taking the fall for Shane. Or worse. The way his mother was acting, however, with the rhythm of her breaths, she was getting close to crying.

"Honey, it's OK." Hearing his father get up from his chair as well, Alex separated to let them embrace. Just in time as well; his throat was tensing up. His thoughts then fell on Bailey. A quick walk with him, even in lieu of the cold outside, felt more desirable right then.

He found Bailey still resting on the futon when he reached the guest room's door. His dog raised his head to look at him within a second. "Hey, boy. Wanna go outside?" Alex asked as he approached. Bailey didn't move or react until he came within a few feet, at which point he stood up and stepped back an inch.

"Bailey, what's wrong?" Alex asked before deciding to hold out his hand for his dog. Bailey took a single glance at it before leaping from the futon and leaving the room. It was the reaction Alex didn't want to see, though he was glad to find Bailey had avoided his room. *Guess I'll leave you alone, then.*

With both his folks and his dog now wary about what was coming, Alex slipped into his room, shut the door behind him, and got back to reading. He took a break from it when he heard his mother knock on his door. By that time, she was dressed and ready to leave for work, and Alex offered her another hug. She asked nothing of him, opting instead for, "I'll see you tonight."

"You will. And I'll be okay."

They then separated, with Alex hoping she wouldn't stay emotional the entire drive. His father, meanwhile, had taken to working on something in the study, judging by the keyboard keys clicking in rapid succession. When Alex checked on him after refilling his water, he found Bailey resting on the couch behind him.

The sounds of the keyboard helped plant in his mind the decision to indulge in one of his older PC titles for a while. It wasn't long before the sounds of an amusement park and rollercoasters filled his room, the pace and appeal of the game making the minutes zip by.

A while later, Alex began to feel a noticeable increase in his pulse. Thinking it was the game and the situation he was in, he paused it and waited. Less than a minute later, not only had his pulse increased instead of decreased, but his fingertips had started going numb.

Then came the taste of fresh blood, and he moved his tongue in time to feel one of his canines lengthen.

The hell? He shot a glance at his desk clock. *8:40? What the hell's going on?* As the first sounds of his claws emerging came, Alex shot up and rushed out of his room. The keyboard in the study was no longer clicking, but he knew his father was in there.

By then, his breathing had changed its pace to match his rapid heartbeat, making him sound winded. His father noticed the instant he appeared in the doorframe, and Bailey once again pulled his head up at the sight of him.

"Alex, what---" his father began before spotting the claws on the hand Alex had pressed to his chest.

"It's happening."

Chapter 7 – ...Gone Awry

Tuesday, October 11th, 2011
Moon Phase – Waxing Gibbous

"Wait, how?" His father got up from his chair as he asked that.

"I don't know. It just is."

His father then turned around. "Bailey, c'mon. Outside."

Bailey obeyed and rushed for the front door. Alex praised him silently and then slipped away before his father followed his dog outside. His jacket and tee were removed first in prep for the crunching up of his stomach, the rest of his clothing--sans his necklace--coming off once he was in his room and the door was shut.

For several worrying seconds, he was left staring at the clawed, shifting hands gripping the foot of his bed frame, and then the pressure hit. As his lungs compressed, several strained grunts were forced out of him, and one of his arms wrapped around his chest.

The quivering of his muscles came soon after. The feeling of it hadn't changed since the first time, still seeming as though someone was digging under his skin and reshaping his muscles, moving him like a puppet against his will.

By the time the compression laxed, his breathing was laced with growls and his tail had begun to emerge. The water left in the nearby glass was chugged down in seconds, though the taste of his blood remained. He made for the bathroom to rinse it out. His limbs, and in effect his steps, were shakier than he expected, forcing him to lean against the walls and then the countertop.

As cold water pooled into his paws, Alex noticed the hints of his fur on them. The itching had yet to start bothering him, but what he knew was coming would.

After several drinks, he returned to his room and lowered himself to the floor. Despite his still-elevated pulse and sweat-drenched skin, he tried to take some easy breaths, only for the Charlie horse rod-through-the-muscles sensations to sweep through his legs. A protracted series of snarls followed as he dug his claws into his carpet and clamped his eyes shut.

Then came the shifting of his ears, and the emergence of the first patches of fur along his spine and back. The subsequent itching ran along his skin like a wave of crawling ants, the rubbing from his paws barely able to counter it. Alex kept trying to catch his breath as it grew in, the fur catching his escaping body heat and driving up his thirst again.

And then he heard bones cracking, first from his skull and jaw, and then from his ribcage.

Resisting the urge to wrap his arms around his chest, Alex flexed his paws as the sounds continued. The first loud snaps of bone came from his ribcage, a series of well over two-dozen of them. As they grew out and then reattached to his sternum, the mental image of his chest being splayed open drew pangs of nausea.

His skull and jaw came next, the localized pain of all the forming cracks giving way to a slack feeling in both bones. His until-now short muzzle then pushed out, forming his longer canine one and allowing his fangs to complete their growth.

The bones had no time to set before the ones in his legs and feet also fractured and snapped. A pair of roaring snarls got away from him before he restrained himself, and his shaky, growl-laced breathing took over again.

Eventually he felt his legs ceasing to reshape, and his breathing began to calm with the last of the stretching. The whole of his body was sore from the shift however and he let his arms slip from his chest and his legs lay as slack as he could allow them.

Before long, his relief was tainted by concern. What had caused him to shift early? He'd been doing nothing unusual or new. He then pictured Shane's werewolf form giving him barely a glance before walking away, an ugly feeling of being slapped in the face following. Why hadn't---

No, fuck him. Alex let a sharp snarl fly before he shook his head and slammed a fist into his carpet. *What help has he been anyway?* His breathing then fully changed to growls for a few seconds, each one releasing some of his pent-up frustration. Once spent, he continued resting on the floor for a while before rolling over and getting to his knees and paws. With his bed frame as a crutch, he pulled himself fully to his feet.

Alex's thoughts returned to his father as he found his footing and let the air conditioning cool him off. He was already hungry and getting ideas about what to have, but letting his father know the shift was over could be done first.

However, he didn't see him near the front door, or within the yard or driveway.

Left to assume both Bailey and his father were in the backyard, a wave of cold soon touched his nerves. Had his father slipped back inside and heard any of the event, or heard him through the window? Or had Bailey kept his hands full the whole time?

After returning to his room and opening his blinds, Alex spotted his father sitting in a chair for the backyard's table, his back to the window. He couldn't tell if he had heard anything, but his gut feeling told him he had. With Bailey nowhere in sight, Alex unlocked the nearest window and slid it up.

His father turned his head at the noise. "Alex?"

Bailey came into view as Alex was about to answer. "Hey, Dad." His voice stopped his dog in his tracks.

"You alright?"

"Sore, but fine."

"Alright. I'm coming back inside."

His father wasted no time doing so, though Bailey was left outside after refusing to come back in. When he stopped near the door to his room and locked eyes on him, Alex gave him a nod just before his stomach started churning. He didn't want to ask and potentially confirm his worries if his father was willing to not say anything.

Once back in the kitchen, Alex pulled some food from the fridge and started with the burgers from the day before. Within minutes they were gone, along with his second choice of leftovers, leaving a glass apiece of water and soda to tide him over as more food was warmed up.

His first few drinks of the fizzing soda drew a hiccup, followed by a growl-laced cough.

"You OK, Son?" his father asked from the study.

"Yeah," Alex replied, though his nostrils were now stinging from the carbonation. His father resumed clicking keys shortly after.

As Alex continued to fill his stomach, he found himself asking what he could do to pass the time until nightfall. He had plenty to read, but could already feel an urge to go outside. The front yard was off-limits, but the backyard... *Hmm. Wouldn't take me more than a few seconds to slip into the garage... Yeah, that'll work.* He then looked towards the kitchen's door to the study. He couldn't see his father minding if he did that, though something urged him to be sure, or at least wait until he had the house to himself.

Nearly an hour from the moment the shift began, Alex's stomach at last felt full. Despite the numerous scents that clung to his fur and pads, he refrained from licking his paws and moved to check on his father. What sounded like PC speaker noises had been coming from the computer for the last few minutes, but he couldn't place them with any program he knew.

Alex received a few seconds' glance when he entered his father's line of sight. To his relief, his father didn't look concerned, and when he spoke, his tone was still neutral. "Something wrong?"

"No. Just finished eating."

His father took a moment before responding. "How long will that last?"

"A while. I can tide myself over with small meals if I need to."

"And what about that other hunger?"

Alex glanced away. No sense in pretending he didn't know. "It hit me a full day into this the first time."

"So, are you saying it'll start affecting you tomorrow morning?"

Alex stopped himself before responding. The shift had happened sooner than he expected. What assurance did he have that his animal hunger would wait a full day? "I don't know. It took eighteen hours the night you and Mom found me like this."

"So, between two and eight a.m., that's the timeframe we're looking at?"

"As far as I can guess."

Alex's father rested his forehead against the fingers of his right hand at that answer, a noticeable sigh following. The noise pushed Alex to close the distance between them and rest a paw on his father's shoulder. At that distance, he could start to hear his father's heartbeat. Faster than he thought, but not by much.

"I won't do anything stupid."

"I know. It's not that."

It's that this is happening at all, isn't it? Alex thought as he tried not to think of Shane. He fought off the build-up of tension in his throat as he patted his father's shoulder, trying not to scratch him.

When he glanced away from his father's face, an MS-DOS-caliber menu above a brightly colored and heavily pixelated background was what he found on the nearby monitor. Hoping the program would serve to lighten the mood, Alex asked, "What's that?"

"It's a game I used to play," his father said after a second.

"Doesn't look familiar."

His father made a slight chuckle and then didn't speak in favor of unpausing the game and getting back to playing. Alex watched as his father typed in commands and guided his avatar around what looked like a spaceship before getting gunned down after a screen change.

"Oh, right. I forgot about him," his father remarked before the game produced a snarky epitaph that made Alex smile.

"It was a good try," Alex replied.

"Think you can do better?" his father asked as he scooted his chair back and got up.

Alex noticed hints of his father's fear scent before he answered. It wasn't strong, but because it was there, his initial response was halted. "Dad, hang on."

His father stopped a few feet behind him. "What?"

Alex hesitated until he turned his head to look behind him. "I'm not making you nervous, am I?"

"I'd be lying if I said no."

Alex sighed as quietly as he could, his eye contact with his father breaking as he did. Shane's words about others trying not to be afraid of him flashed through his mind a second later, though he couldn't help wondering if in this instance, the scent was emerging for a reason other than his presence.

"I don't know what else to tell you."

"It's fine. Maybe time will help temper that." Alex got no response. His father simply waited a few seconds before resuming his walk towards the kitchen.

Chapter 8 – Away The Hours

Tuesday, October 11th, 2011
Moon Phase – Waxing Gibbous

As he waited for his father to return, Alex started a new game and quickly found himself hunting and pecking keys to type out the commands he needed. His first few discoveries came easily, until a series of incorrect commands stopped him.

"You stuck?" his father asked after circling around to his right side.

"Yeah. Don't know why, though."

His father hummed. "Use 'look' instead."

Alex did so and was greeted with a new prompt. "Oh."

His father chuckled. "Sometimes it's not the word you think."

"I'll remember that," Alex said before finishing his business and directing the avatar out of the room. Once the next screen appeared, the same enemy emerged and killed him.

Stuck between surprise and a fit of laughter at the outcome, his father had time to respond. "Well, good try."

Alex then stepped aside from the chair and his father retook his seat. Immediately after, what he'd meant to ask before was back on his mind, along with Bailey. *Better let him back in.*

He found his dog resting with his back to the sliding glass door. Before disturbing him, Alex found the garage keys in the nearby table, figuring if his father trusted him enough to not do anything stupid, using the garage as an outdoor refuge wouldn't violate that trust.

Bailey snapped to attention, and then recoiled from Alex's form when the glass was tapped. "It's okay, boy." He then slid the door open, prompting Bailey to back up further, and was about to step aside for him when he heard his phone sound the IM received tone.

In his haste to return to his room and read it, Alex forgot how useless his claws and pads were for working with a touchscreen. After finding a stylus and unlocking the phone, he found that Nathan had messaged him, with Marcus and Catherine in the same chat room.

Nathan T.: You doing okay, man?

Alex heard Bailey come inside and walk past his open door as he typed up his response.

Alex S.: Yeah. It already happened, though.

Expecting any replies to take a while, Alex made his way back to the glass door. The hundreds of scents from outside had swept over more than half the room already, and despite the disorientation from his brain processing them so quickly, the novelty of them compared to the stuffiness of his room was an instant stress reliever. Now he wanted to be outside more than anything.

He hesitated at the door for a moment before dropping to all fours and then making a beeline for the garage door. As soon as it was opened, he slipped inside, into the pool of other familiar scents the door had kept bottled. His nearby grindbox then became an impromptu bench, first for sitting and then for resting, as the morning breezes cycled scents in and out of the garage.

The IM tone sounded a short time later. This time, Marcus responded.

Marcus A.: Seriously?

Alex S.: Yeah. Caught me by surprise.

After pressing "send", Alex switched to his phone's video player. He chuckled silently at the outburst moments from the video he chose, pausing it only to check another text.

Marcus A.: Your folks weren't there, I hope.

Alex S.: Mom wasn't. Dad and Bailey
didn't see it, thankfully.

The minutes ticked by without a response from either Nathan or Marcus, and for a moment, Catherine's silence drew concern. *Eh, she's probably busy.* After a few more videos, Alex sat back up and stared into the barely lit garage.

An urge to go beyond the backyard, to the wooded lot across the street, had been rising for the last few minutes. He was already out here, and he'd heard few cars coming or going since coming outside.

He shook his head before the thought progressed further. He wasn't about to risk being seen by a civilian or betray his father's trust. It took several minutes of reaffirming that for the urge to go away, by which time he was growing thirsty.

After looking inside to be sure his parents' bedroom was empty, Alex opened the door only to hear footsteps coming towards the room. The door was closed, and his back was turned when his father entered the room.

There was silence for a moment, and then, "Were you thinking of going outside?"

How neutral his father's tone was erased Alex's urge to lie to him. "Coming back inside, actually. Just hung out in the garage for a little while."

"Oh. Was that something you did the first time this happened?"

"Sort of. I just had a window open that time."

His father hummed in response.

"It made me a little stir-crazy, being stuck inside, but the garage seems to work fine."

His father nodded. "Good to know."

When Alex began to move, his father stepped aside, though not far enough to avoid a pat on the shoulder from one of his paws as he passed.

Before long, morning had given way to afternoon, the increased intensity of the sunlight tempering Alex's desires to go back outside. He left one of his bedroom windows open to compensate and resigned himself to reading, the size and shape of his paws making the mass-market-sized books he owned harder to hold and turn only one page of.

He changed his focus to rolling handfuls of dice after some time, smiling when the dice turned up good numbers. His imagination then trailed into having his friends around a table, himself as game master while they had books, character sheets, snacks and more spread out around themselves.

That would be perfect right about now.

Chapter 9 - The Company of Friends

Tuesday, October 11th, 2011
Moon Phase – Waxing Gibbous

As the time ticked over to 1:30 p.m. and his father awoke from the nap he was taking in his room, Alex's phone sounded its IM tone.

Nathan T.: If you're bored, do you
want to go a few rounds with me?

Although his friend didn't elaborate, Alex knew what he was implying. It was when he reached for his keyboard that he was reminded of how big his clawed fingers were compared to his human ones. He then tested their positions and found them striking two or three keys by default. Nothing some key rebinding couldn't fix, though his friend would still have some advantage over him.

He sat on things for a minute before answering.

Alex S.: Yeah, sure. Why not?

Nathan T.: Give me until 2:30 then.
Gotta do something first.

That gives me less than an hour. Alex spent most of that time getting used to how it felt mashing keys to move his avatar around. After a while, he began questioning removing the other keys and leaving just the ones he needed.

He shook his head after staring at his keyboard for a moment. It would make things far easier, but picking the thing apart for one game? The idea of a second keyboard just for that purpose quickly became more appealing and stuck in his mind longer.

It was nearing 2:15 p.m. when Alex heard heavy footsteps and the jingling of metal behind him. He turned and found his father dressed in his police uniform, ready to leave but looking like something was on his mind.

"Before I go, I want to know what your plans are for tonight." There was a cautious yet direct edge to his father's tone.

Alex broke eye contact. He hadn't given that much thought. All that was crucial to him was the hunger, and if he was correct in his assumptions, it wouldn't surface until well into the night.

To his relief, his father didn't say his name as he thought of how to reply. "I guess keep doing what I have been: keep myself occupied."

"What about where you're planning on going?"

Alex glanced at his father. The ranch where he'd encountered Shane came to mind first, then the stable at his high school, then the animal farm near Marcus and Catherine's neighborhood. All three of them would be easier to hit late at night, if not after midnight, but all that his high school's stable had left were big animals.

"I think the ranch that Shane was at before." Alex saw no hints of disagreement when he looked at his father again. Likely a good sign.

"Then whatever you do, or have to do, either tonight or tomorrow, I want you to remember to put your safety ahead of everything else." The shift in his father's tone was evident from his first words. Concern had overtaken the cautious angle.

"I will. I won't forget."

His father nodded. "Then I'll see you tomorrow."

"Likewise, Dad."

As his father walked away, and then left the house altogether, Alex took a moment before returning his focus to the game. He was working his way through its single-player maps when his phone rang, making him jump at the noise. It was Nathan.

"Hello?" Alex said after the speaker option was turned on.

"Hey, man." Nathan's voice was a welcome sound to hear. "You ready?"

"More or less. Let's do this."

With his phone serving as the stand in for a microphone, the two of them began the first deathmatch round. Despite the binding tweaks, Alex still found his claws scratching and getting stuck between keys, and Nathan was quick to gain several frags off him.

A short growl got away from him when he was killed within seconds of respawning. The smack talk Nathan had been throwing his way halted for a short time in response. "I'm okay," Alex said after he realized it.

"So, this…" Nathan paused to pay attention to the rocket barrage Alex was raining down on him. Several exploded near him, sapping the life from his avatar. "Damn it."

Gotcha. "What was that?" Alex asked after he finished pumping the arm controlling the mouse.

"I was asking if this is the most entertainment you've had all day."

Alex evaded Nathan's chaingun fire before he answered. "So far."

"So, what happened?" Nathan asked after he claimed another frag.

"No idea. This just happened with no warning."

"That guy didn't tell you?"

Alex growled instead of scoffing. "No. Haven't seen him since Friday, in fact."

"Well, maybe he finally got the hint that you don't want him around."

Alex decided not to let his friend know about the scent-marking. "Doubt it, but so long as he doesn't touch you guys or my folks, fine by me."

The deathmatches continued between them for several more rounds, with Nathan saying near the start of the last one, "I gotta stop after this one. Got some homework to do."

"I get you," Alex replied. He continued once the game was over and his phone was in his paw. "Thanks a lot, man. That was fun." His friend hung up one reply later, and once his computer was shut down, the house was left quiet once again.

Alex then returned to the book he'd been reading, only to notice Bailey poking his head inside the room and staring at him. "Hey, boy." His dog didn't move. "You want outside, right?" Despite further inaction from Bailey, Alex got up and started opening the doors to lead him out back. His dog hesitated to move closer to the last one until Alex stood far enough aside, at which point he zipped outside.

At first, Alex meant to close the door and check on him later. A few seconds of standing by an exit from the house changed his mind, and he followed his dog outside. The garage was still unlocked and, as before, he left it unlit and lay down on his grindbox, letting his nose take in the scents within the building. Several dozen new scents had appeared since morning, some piquing his interest as to their source. The few human scents he noticed were too weak to belong to anyone nearby, and no nearby noises revealed the presence of others.

After some time, he heard Bailey's claws clicking on the concrete within the garage. They stopped near the door and even without looking, Alex could tell Bailey was staring at him, despite the unlit space hiding him.

"It's me, boy. You're alright," Alex said as he sat back up. His dog backpedaled out of the garage before he took a single step and didn't follow him into the house until he was back in his own room. By then, the thought of a real nap was growing in appeal, and Alex left his door open in case Bailey wanted to try and approach him.

* * *

When he woke, two hours had gone by and the sun was starting to set, its lower angle flooding his room with bright yellow light. Little more than two hours remained before night would arrive.

Alex took his time sitting up and stretching, and noted some of the new scents swirling around his room. Someone upwind was burning charcoal, and cooking what smelled like lean ground beef. Scents that put his returning hunger back in mind.

As he slid off his bed, Alex was once again startled by the ringing of his phone. It was Marcus this time.

"Hello?"

"Hey. Did you get my text?"

Alex then ran his stylus down the screen. There was a text there, from half an hour ago.

Marcus A.: Would you mind us
stopping by for a few minutes?

"Yeah. I just saw it, though. It came in while I was sleeping."

"Alright. Are you okay with that then?"

"Sure. Come by whenever you want."

"Will do."

As his friend hung up, Alex was left to wonder who Marcus was bringing along with him. Just Catherine was his best guess.

Once in the kitchen, he warmed up a whole package of hot dogs and nipped at their lengths when they cooled. In the middle of the fourth one, he began hearing a truck's engine traveling up the driveway. His quick peek outside revealed the red truck Marcus drove, and both him and Catherine in the vehicle cabin.

He didn't keep watch to see if both of them were coming; just having them nearby was enough to perk him up.

When the knocking on the door came, Alex heard Bailey leap off whatever he was resting on and rush for the door. His enthusiasm and pace were halted upon seeing his werewolf form, at which time Alex reached for the doorknob and inched the front door open, keeping behind it as he did so.

Pleasant and familiar food scents swept inside immediately, and although he tried not to focus on the potential sources as Marcus and then Catherine entered, his few glances confirmed it was Chick-Fil-A. His friends had clear reservation in their expressions, which he expected, but nonetheless felt a twinge of concern from seeing.

Marcus spoke first as the door was closed, the deadbolt left unlocked. "Hey, man."

Alex glanced back at them. Already, Bailey was begging for attention, his tail wagging rapidly as Catherine coaxed him over to be petted. "Hey. Thanks for stopping by."

"No problem."

Alex glanced at the take-out bag again, then at Bailey and Catherine. Seeing him so happy was a nice change.

"Oh, right. This." Marcus held out the paper bag. "Thought you'd like it, even if just for a snack."

"Always do. Thanks, Marcus." Alex took the bag before speaking again. "You guys can sit in the kitchen if you want."

"It's fine. We won't be here long."

Upon hearing that, Alex briefly regretted his choice to have a nap. "Plans for tonight?"

"Somewhat."

"Then so long as it's not studying, have fun."

Marcus only nodded, then reached down to pet Bailey's head. Things stayed quiet between the three of them for a time, until Catherine broke the silence. "What about you?"

At first, Alex thought she was referring to how his day had gone. Before he replied, he caught himself and wondered if she meant what was coming, either tonight or tomorrow. "A bit concerned, to be honest."

"About that thing, right?" Marcus asked.

"Yeah," Alex said after letting an exhale out through his nose. "About when it'll happen, mostly."

"When it'll happen?"

"Yeah. The first time it came a full day had passed, and then I had to wait until night to deal with it. I won't have that chance this time if it happens after eight-forty in the morning."

Alex's reply left both his friends without words for a minute.

"Are you sure it has to be then?" Marcus eventually asked.

"It feels like it, but no, I'm not." Shane's face flashed through his head again. "Plus, Shane's been AWOL since I confronted him last Friday, and he never told me anything."

Marcus hummed. "Maybe it's me, but when I think 'hunger', I think of a need that hasn't been satisfied."

Alex glanced at Catherine, but she provided no response. "Now that you mention it, I have only reacted to that hunger."

"My point exactly. What if it's like any other need? A get it over with early and you're done kind of thing?"

Alex held his muzzle in one paw. His friend's logic was sound, but after a few seconds, something started to worry him. What if that wasn't possible, and he had no choice but to wait?

"Plus, like you said, you've been reacting to it. This time, you know it's coming."

Alex was too fixated on the potential lose-lose facing him to respond.

"What's wrong?" Catherine asked.

"This feeling that it's not that easy," Alex replied after a slow sigh. More silence followed.

"I still think it's your best option, man," Marcus said. "If you try and do it tomorrow morning, you'll be cutting things really close."

"I know." When his friends stayed quiet, he continued. "I'm not holding you guys up, am I?"

Catherine shook her head.

"No," Marcus replied. "We do have to head out soon, though."

"Alright. Before you do, thanks for the food and the willing ears."

"No problem."

Alex smiled in return and his friends left soon after, with some parting words to stay safe. "I will, I promise," Alex had replied before they closed the door behind themselves. He then watched them leave through the glass of the door, glad to have spent even a few minutes with them.

Chapter 10 – Off the Familiar Path

Tuesday, October 11th, 2011
Moon Phase – Waxing Gibbous

By then, the scents from the takeout bag were starting to make him hungry. Bailey followed at a distance as he headed for the kitchen, much to his amusement. *You ignore me if I toss you treats, yet you're curious about this. Silly dog.* He emptied the contents onto a plate, then restrained himself from taking more than nibbles at a time.

As he ate, his mind stayed on what was to come. He wanted to believe Marcus was right, but if he made no plans for if it wasn't, he was just as screwed. Hunting twice would be a waste of an animal, along with putting him at risk of being seen. Could he hide his kill somewhere and recover it later? He knew that worked with actual wolves.

Alex paused his eating a moment later. As though a switch had been flipped, the answer nearly blinked into his head. If he stole his kill and brought it home, the only issues he would have would be storing the carcass until he needed it, and where to dump it afterward. A smile grew across his muzzle at the realization, and a measure of weight lifted from his chest as he returned to eating.

When he finished, his first concern was how wide of a selection the ranch had. The doe he'd eaten a considerable amount of flesh from versus the raccoon, but he'd gone hungry for longer the first time, and the raccoon couldn't have been more than seven or eight pounds. He strained his memory for the animal scents he'd noticed that day, recalling some from goats, horses, and pigs. The pigs felt like the easiest pickings, and he'd noticed at least four of their scents before.

How heavy do those things get? After some searching on his phone, he was left hoping there were some juveniles to pick from. Anything bigger would be a waste of meat, or near impossible to lift out of any enclosure, much less onto his shoulders once it was down.

41

That still leaves the goats... He winced at the thought of what that animal's meat would taste like before wondering how late he should wait before leaving the house. He tossed ideas around a bit before settling on 9:30. If the walk to the ranch took as long as the walk to his high school, it would be past 10:00 when he arrived. Late enough to make his trek back that much easier.

Okay...how can I preserve that meat? Alex was quick to imagine using one of the coolers in the garage. He could get ice from the refrigerator no problem, but the carcass would have to be wrapped in something to help keep it fresh and keep the cooler from being stained with blood. *A trashbag should do the job.*

Alex returned to his room and settled back into reading as the sun set, the outside winds continuing to mix new scents into his room. A pair of fantasy novels he'd yet to touch made it into his paws for a chapter each, along with a few new comics. Eventually he made his way into the garage, picked out what he needed, and filled his chosen cooler with ice. The amount he got was barely enough for a one cube layer over the bottom. Enough, he hoped, to last until 9:00 a.m. tomorrow.

* * *

When his mother returned home, the sound of her car's engine coming up the driveway reached both him and Bailey. His dog leapt off the guest room futon within seconds and ran for the front door. Alex didn't follow in favor of moving to sit atop his bed.

When his mother appeared in his doorway, he was relieved to see her expression and body lacking tension. Her tone, however, was laced with bottled-up concern. "Did everything go okay?"

Alex was left assuming his father told her what happened. "Yeah. No problems."

"You changed early, though."

"Yeah, but it was alright. Dad and Bailey got outside."

His mother waited a few seconds. "Nothing else?"

"Not yet."

She held her response again. "Whenever it happens...stay safe."

Oh, man. Alex glanced away for a second. "I will. I have been."

"Then, I'll see you in the morning. Love you."

"You too, Mom." After his mother walked away, Alex made for the kitchen. He was getting peckish, though didn't completely fill his stomach. One hour remained until he planned to leave, and if he returned home to find normal food unable to satisfy his stomach, then his prey would serve its purpose.

As that hour ticked by, his attention was split between his book and the noises coming from his parent's bedroom. His mother went to bed not long after entering the room, though it wasn't until close to 9:00 p.m. that the light sawing sound of snoring reached his ears.

Time then seemed to slow as Alex put his book aside and attempted to focus on what was coming. He checked on Bailey once before 9:30, finding him resting on the couch in the living room. Shortly after, he grew curious if Shane was watching the house, and glanced outside through the glass on the front door. Though he did notice something moving within the wooded lot after a minute, it was quickly revealed to be a dark-furred pitbull.

Alex kept an eye on the dog as it wandered and then left the lot. It eventually took the road running south instead of east, much to his relief. After a few more minutes to be sure it wouldn't turn around, he crept back towards his room. By then his mother's snoring was more pronounced, and after a few second's glance at the guest room window, he made his move.

The sliding noises the window made with each movement briefly masked the snoring, and once outside, with how quiet things around him were, Alex made his way to the backyard gate; jumping the fence would be too noisy, he felt. Once the latch was up, he inched the gate open, staying low and near his mother's sedan as he did so. Maintaining his canine stance after the gate was closed, he began his trek down the street. Twice he was forced to hide from passing vehicles, the second one's high beams coming close to lighting him up.

Eventually, the creek was in sight. He hustled towards it as soon as the coast was clear and slid down the bank, slipping under the bridge right after to catch his breath and relax his pulse. Once he'd reached the end of the creek, Alex took a moment to scan the area. Everything was quiet and still and lit up by the moon. Unlike last month, the skatepark was empty.

Hmm. I could dump the carcass around here. Doubt anything besides carrion birds would notice. As he looked around for a good spot, Alex recalled finding Shane's scent in the fields near his middle school. Curious if he had already come around, once across the bridge over the drainage basin, Alex lowered his head and retraced his steps from his first night. This time he found no hints of Shane's scent, and resumed his trek once he was satisfied.

The sidewalk he followed eventually led to another bridge, this one just north of the local library. The steel rods set into the concrete structure's undersides were what drew his attention most, and up close, he found he could barely slip between any two of them. *Shouldn't slow me down too much. What's the traffic density around here, though?*

After settling into a position on the south crest of the bank, Alex snuck a peek over it. The trees to his right were unilluminated except when headlights passed by, and the median between the roads was also unlit thanks to a burnt-out streetlamp. Within what felt like thirty seconds however, seven vehicles had driven over the bridge. *I'll barely have four seconds at a time... No, too risky.*

He slipped back down the bank and then between the bars, the brightness of the lights on the other side, and how much of the basin they lit up, pushing him to wait. *Traffic's going north. If I stay close to the bank...* A sudden squealing of tires, and then the double blip of a police siren, caused his pulse to jump and tore his attention from his planning. When the walls he could see above the bank flashed red and blue, his legs turned to lead. *Oh, perfect. Where's it stopping?*

As the cruiser drove over the bridge, the flashing lights he could see moved further north, fading until little hint of them was left. His assumption that the officer had made a right-hand turn urged him down onto all fours before moving again. His still-racing heart got the old feeling of many eyes on him to resurface, and until he felt fully hidden in the darkness, it didn't subside.

The next road he came to, after avoiding the spotlights of an active baseball and football field, wasn't devoid of dedicated lights either, but after a minute of watching, he crossed it on all fours and slipped into the treeline just beyond it. The darkness the trees provided got him up and walking again, with the occasional pause to listen for strange noises not revealing anything along the way. At least nothing louder than the crickets surrounding him.

As the first hints of the ranch began to show beyond the trees, a shift in the breeze swept the animal scents past his muzzle. The place was housing at least three horses, seven pigs, and four goats. More than enough to choose from.

But along with the animal scents came others. Several belonging to car engines, and others belonging to leather, metal lubricant, and gunpowder.

Alex's pulse rose within a second of noticing the last one, and his legs almost unwillingly lowered him into a crouch, the crunching of dried leaves sounding much louder than any time before.

Although he heard no footsteps anywhere ahead of him, he didn't dare move. The animal scents were sapped of their previously hopeful edge at the same time, leaving him dreading any sudden signals of hunger or being spotted and having to flee.

His high school's stable suddenly felt much safer than here, but only for a moment. What if the police were watching that location too?

The foal should still be there... That idea was gradually tossed as he thought back over his route to get there. Unless he weakened the animal somehow, if he lost his grip on it...

Alex snapped his head to his left in shock when grassy steps sounded behind him, then bolted left, keeping on all fours and not looking back. He didn't stop until he was out of the cluster of trees. By then, his pulse was so accelerated and his stance so wobbly, any sense he had of being hidden was dashed.

And then he heard it coming his direction.

He inched back, keeping parallel to the treeline. How many were following him? Could he fool them at this point by acting like a dog?

Can't act aggress---shit, my necklace. Alex almost didn't resist reaching for it.

He inched back further and then looked down at his paws. He couldn't disguise that hand-like shape, could he? After tucking his thumbs under his palms, the abnormal length and mass were still noticeable.

Alex fought the urge to flee back the way he'd come. He was faster than whoever was following him---more mobile too, with the bulk if he needed it. His back arched, almost by itself, and his body braced for a decision to move.

It was then that he began to see a dark, animal-looking mass coming closer between the trees. When it stood up and he could see some tan fur, he eased only briefly.

Shane said nothing as he emerged from the treeline. He continued to be silent as he went down to all fours again, his expression doing all the talking once Alex made it out. "The hell was that?" summed it up.

At the same time, Alex became lost in questioning how he'd not noticed Shane before now. Or smelled him. Had he been followed? Or had Shane been hiding somewhere nearby and he'd not noticed?

When Shane broke eye contact with him, his attention seeming to change to the trees nearby, Alex followed suit, wondering if someone was close. He heard nothing but did see Shane's left paw lift some. He then gestured for him to come closer, but Alex ignored it and didn't budge, even when Shane shot him a look seconds later.

Shane's head turned one more time towards the trees before he began closing the distance between them. A single step back was all Alex got before Shane was within breathing distance of him, his ears folding back and his head tucking some in turn.

"Guess you had the same idea I did," Shane said, keeping his voice down.

"I can't risk it," Alex replied, the calmness of Shane's voice delaying his response for a moment.

"I figured."

"Could be the police."

"It could..." Shane looked around some, then tossed his head. "Back that way. Circle around and check." Alex hesitated again, slowly turning his head to look behind him. "You want me to do it?"

"No. I'll do it."

Shane looked over him briefly. "If it is them, we can wait them out."

"Maybe."

Chapter 11 – Hunting Under Pressure

Tuesday, October 11th, 2011
Moon Phase – Waxing Gibbous

Alex took a breath to relax his nerves before turning around. The length of the treeline went on for a way, the edge brightly lit by the full moon and the shadows leaning to his right. After a few steps he thought to cross into the treeline before moving closer but decided against it shortly after; how unfamiliar everything was and what could be awaiting him and Shane nearby made the option with less noise potential better.

When he glanced back around the halfway point, Alex no longer saw Shane and halted. *The hell? Where'd he go?* He kept still for a moment before hearing rustling and crunching grass noises moving away from his position, further into the brush jungle that he'd refused to go into.

Figuring Shane was moving to a safer spot out of eyesight of others, after thinking he was moving to check on the ranch as well, just in a riskier way, Alex resumed his trek. *If the police are watching that ranch, which way are they facing?* He pulled what memory he had of the satellite images of the ranch before settling on west-facing as the most likely.

He drew closer to the edge of the treeline, keeping an eye on the thickness of the brush for any gaps he could look through. The ditch and clearing he was approaching were illuminated by passing vehicle headlights. From his position, he could see the beams light up all the clearing past the treeline's end.

Patrolling officers, if not the ranch owner, were next on his mind. They'd likely have flashlights. Reducing his pace to little more than a creep, alert for the slightest odd or close noise beyond his paws and body meeting vegetation, Alex dropped to his chest as another vehicle came closer, this time from his left. Once again, the headlights lit up more of the clearing than he was comfortable with.

Better make this fast. He rounded the edge of the treeline shortly after that thought, his initial view of the path towards the ranch showing no sign of the police. It wasn't until almost all of it was visible that the shape of an SUV became noticeable, and then the color scheme, the lights, and the outline of the word "POLICE". Even worse was the direction it, and the officer inside, were facing: northwest.

Alex had no chance to reign in his unease from the discovery before the officer in the cruiser turned his head to his right, and then stopped.

Certain he'd been spotted, Alex froze instead of backing away, his attention locked on the officer and any moves he made. His shoulder radio was reached for, and then the vehicle's door lock was popped.

That sound snapped Alex from his frozen posture, and he retreated behind the treeline as footsteps on gravel sounded and a stream of light hit the spot where he'd been just a second before. A stream too intense to be from a flashlight. *Shit, that was close.*

His expectation that Shane would reemerge after seeing the beam was proven true as he kept pacing along the edge of the treeline. He could hear him coming from the twigs and leaves he was crushing, though his stance, and the demeanor he showed, put to rest Alex's other thoughts of being belittled. "They see you?"

Alex looked back. "Not with that."

Shane's response hum came as a light growl. "Stay close."

Though at first not wanting to, with another look back towards where the beam had hit, Alex followed him back a ways, and then into the vegetation. How much darker it was after several steps eased his anxiety a touch, and he got back to his hind paws as Shane had already done.

With a bit of an idea where he was being led, Alex soon saw the western edge of the ranch through the trees. The southmost enclosure building hid most of the cruiser from the direction they were approaching, but how well-lit everything was made the idea of getting a kill of any kind without raising an alarm feel near impossible.

Cutting the power, leaving and trying somewhere else, distracting the officer--somehow--before going for it... All of those ideas were turned over in Alex's head as he moved close to the same holly bush Shane was using, opting to crouch instead of going to all fours. Although certain Shane had also thought about at least one of those options, how still he was when he next glanced over at him made him hold his tongue for a moment.

"Now what?" he finally asked. Shane only gave him a glance. With little beyond the crickets around them making any noise, Alex inched around his edge of the bush to check on what was holding Shane's attention. The only animal pen he could see that was exposed from his angle was the pig pen. The planks and rods of its several-foot-high wooden fence were shielded with wire mesh, and at least two pigs were sleeping outside the makeshift shelter.

Is he seriously... Alex's heart began to race. How intent Shane seemed was enough to keep it going at that pace. What he would have to do if the hunger suddenly emerged, and what Shane might do, officer or not, if it did were next on his mind. *No, calm down. He said we could wait them out.*

After forcing his thoughts back onto how they could make getting to the animals easier, Alex glanced around what was visible of the ranch, noting anything that seemed important. While doing so, he almost missed the hints of headlights and grinding of stones near the already-sitting police cruiser. He then checked on Shane, who didn't seem fazed, but swore at himself for not being more careful.

When the second vehicle stopped and the first hint of voices reached him, Alex almost inched forward before closing his eyes and cupping a paw behind his left ear. "Didn't really see it," was the first thing he fully heard.

Oh, thank God.

"Too big for a coyote, though." The ounce of pleasure Alex got from those words faded as it became evident that the second cruiser wasn't leaving, and it took the brushing of grass where Shane stood to open his eyes and pull his attention away.

Not once did he break a twig or be any louder than the insects around them for longer than a split second as he crept away from the bush, briefly reviving Alex's fears of his friends being stalked. When Shane then shot him a glance, he didn't dare move. Only turn his eyes away. Alex then took another look at the ranch, giving Shane enough time to get closer and tap his shoulder.

"Now what?" Alex asked in response, his nervous tone clear.

"We wait, and get what we can, when we can."

Alex gave Shane only a second of eye-contact before shaking his head.

"Got a better idea?"

"We leave. Try somewhere else."

"Not that high school."

That was quick. "Why?"

"You haven't been over there lately, have you?" The annoyance in Shane's tone got Alex thinking it was a newly installed security system, or permanently stationed security guard. "There's no animals over there anymore."

Alex looked back toward Shane when he heard that, his surprise fading after a second. Two dead animals within a month would've prompted that.

"Wasn't my idea," Alex said after a bit of quiet.

"What was?"

"An animal farm, north of here."

Shane looked past him, then shook his head. "We're already here."

"And it's being watched, by the police."

"Then tell me, is that other place not?" Alex held his tongue after meeting Shane's gaze again, feeling more angry than off-guard. "Never crossed your mind to check, did it?"

Alex exhaled in favor of letting out a few choice words. "What are we watching for, then?"

Shane leaned up and looked over the brush, then crouched back down before answering. "One less cruiser. Then," he threw his head to the right, "him being distracted."

Alex mimicked the lean up to check on things as well. The original officer looked busy with his cruiser's laptop. *That can't be enough.* As he dropped back to all fours, he echoed that thought aloud.

"If you're fast enough, it will be."

Alex could feel his heart speed up at those words. Could he be that quick? Much less grab something and not lose it? Shane's shaking head then pulled his attention back to him. "What?"

"You're panicking already."

"And you're not?"

"If this is all it takes to make you freeze and second guess things, you will go hungry."

Alex diverted his gaze for a second, his parents flashing to mind. "Then forgive me for not being so cold-blooded," he retorted, a weak growl accompanying his words.

Shane shook his head again, slow enough that it made him seem like a disapproving family member. For a while after, neither of them wanted to fully break eye-contact; Shane did so only to get another look at the ranch.

After several more minutes, there came the sound of an engine turning over. While Shane inched around the bush at the sound, Alex stayed put, opting to lean up again. The original cruiser was backing up, likely to leave. The realization eased some of the tension throughout his chest and limbs, more so as he considered the possible field of view of the new officer. He was parked further south, still facing half that way and half west, and the nearby horse stable was lined up well with his cruiser's windshield.

When Alex next glanced towards Shane, only half of his hind legs were visible. He dropped back to all fours and followed him, stopping when it was clear Shane wasn't moving beyond the barbed wire and wood pole fence. For a few moments, all Shane did was stare out towards the pigs, then his head turned to look behind him, Alex's gaze meeting his.

Now what? Expecting Shane to come back his way and then dictate to him what animal was his, he braced for another verbal match.

The words he heard instead once Shane was close caused his body heat to seep from his skin and though his pelt. "You go first."

Alex glanced to his left once, his jaws separating ever slightly. The question of why was immediately on his mind, but he couldn't say even that.

"If you go after me," Shane said after a length of silence, "you'll just panic even more, and then one or both of us are screwed."

Most of Shane's words barely pierced Alex's already worry-laden mindset. Did he not care if he was seen? Alex closed his eyes and sighed, feeling his heart racing under his skin, and once again imagined cutting the power to the ranch's lights. It was so simple an idea that it stayed swirling in his thoughts, and in turn made what he saw happening if either of them was seen even more agitating and worrying.

When he again glanced in the direction of the pig pen, then up towards the lights of the ranch, Shane took advantage of his silence. "If you can't do it, then go. Use that other place if that'll calm you down."

"I can't be a little concerned?"

"Visibly shaking is a little concerned?"

Alex exhaled. "What's your plan if he sees you?"

"Don't panic, get what I want, and leave. The same thing I've always done." Shane continued after a second. "Why? You think he's going to pull his gun the instant he sees one of us?"

Alex swallowed at that statement and reached for his necklace as his ears laid back. Shane continued before he could speak.

"Cops don't do that. Your dad's a cop. Have you ever known him to do that?"

Alex shook his head, his necklace and bullet still grasped in his right paw.

"Then stop stressing out and quit worrying about me while you're at it. Get what you want, then I'll get what I want. Done."

The question Alex wanted to ask, which animal Shane was eying, refused to leave his lungs, even after he closed his eyes again and took a few breaths to calm himself. The pigs were the most exposed. So long as he had a firm grip... But if he didn't kill the animal quickly, the squealing would reveal where he was fleeing, and if the officer called for backup and sent cars his direction...

The animal farm returned to mind, but so did Shane's words. If that place was also being watched, he'd arrive long after Shane had caused every officer within ten miles to be on alert for something like him. If two separate incidents occurred the same night... Or what if they brought out the canine units?

With that train of thought, Alex opened his eyes. He met Shane's gaze for just a moment; the loss of the curl-up of his muzzle and lips was obvious, though his stare was still as unmoving as ever. It made Alex's first steps to the south, and around him, slow and cautions.

While wishing the evening breezes would, even for a second, blow west or southwest again instead of just south, he kept inching along until he heard Shane start to follow him. He glanced back, but Shane said nothing. It took a few minutes at his current pace to start to see the rear of the new cruiser, the moon helping light up the words "K9 Unit" on its rear.

His frustrated response huff pulled a response from Shane, albeit a hushed one. "What?"

Alex looked back at him but stayed silent until he was closer. "Canine unit."

"Don't let that bother you." Shane replied. "He won't just let the dog go and, for all we know, he's napping."

Alex took a few seconds to think before siding with Shane's logic. Even so, the possibility of having to fight such a trained animal made his stomach turn. On his way back to the ranch, and the barbed wire fence, Shane continued to keep close. The position of the cruiser was still a concern, and Alex couldn't help thinking about how he could keep an eye on it without exposing too much of his head. There weren't any easily accessible, much less useful, reflective things nearby, and going around to the other side would just bring him directly into the officer's line of sight.

Asking Shane to watch for when he could make a move... If he was seen, or got the officer to start looking around, it would be for nothing. Was his best option really just to go for it? All he could see if he did was a window of three, at most five seconds to run for it and jump the pig pen fence, after which the officer would call for backup.

He tossed those numbers around for a bit, and then something clicked. He looked back at Shane, who was closing in on him, and then spoke. "What if I got one big enough for both of us? Removed the chance of you being seen?" To his surprise, Shane shook his head. "Why not? It makes perfect sense to me."

"Not if we're trying to be fast. Get a smaller one, and then get out."

Alex didn't want to fully agree, but his drive to argue was starting to dissipate. No other ideas came to him, even as he took another look at the pig pen. How tight his stomach was made the idea of eating any of what was just across from him even more unpleasant.

After another handful of breaths, he took hold of the nearby wooden pole. With a hop and a thrust of his arms, he was over the barbed wire, his paws making little more than a 'phut' against the dirt. Behind him, Shane drew closer on two legs. He heard his claws scratch the head of the wooden pole.

Opting to stay on all fours, Alex sized up the pen, his heart once again starting to race. The fence was about four feet high. Clearable, but the gate and padlock would make noise if he vaulted over at that point. Several yards separated him from the pen, a distance he felt he could clear within two or three seconds. All that was keeping him rooted was the officer. How could he tell if the officer was distracted, or was Shane expecting him to consider what he was seeing before acting?

That Shane was expecting the officer to stay in the cruiser instead of getting out was what Alex settled on. With his breaths starting to sound shaky, he leaned forward and stretched out a paw, his eyes darting between the edge of the stable and the pig pen. At the very least, he was thankful that Shane was not trying to get him to move.

He took three more breaths, each working as part of a countdown, and then with a thrust of his back legs, took off.

His claws tore into and threw up the dirt he ran over as his body, his heart, his head, and his lungs started to race. The gate was closing in fast, and as he came close, he tilted his head up and leapt for it. The padlock jimmied as the gate was pushed back, and then he was diving onto the group of enclosed pigs.

The one his paws connected with was a small one, but once it was jolted awake and began to squeal, its weight seemed to double. Then the others started squealing, the noise tearing into Alex's ears and getting his teeth to grit. At once, he felt like every eye within a mile was on him, and then his grip slipped.

He lunged at the piglet, catching it again and digging his claws between its ribcage and into its neck and shoulders. After shaking his head to fight the piercing noises, he focused on the shelter the rest were running around. Its top was solid wood, enough to hold his weight, and the fence was just...

That was when he heard the canine unit start barking. With the piglet held as tight as his left paw and arm would allow, he leapt atop the shelter, the animal's thrashing hooves raking at his chest and arm, and yanking fur all the while. As he cleared the fence and dropped into the brush, Alex reclaimed his grip, this time grabbing the piglet by the head and clamping its snout. The scent of its blood was already reaching his muzzle, causing his stomach to relax, but until he heard Shane reach the gate, and then the officer calling for backup, he didn't move.

Shane was out of the pen four seconds later, his choice of pig held not only by the neck in his muzzle, but with both paws. As Alex looked back at him, the piglet began to twitch, and his grip was tested again. Almost without thinking, he parted his jaws and tried to get his fangs into the piglet's neck as he picked up his pace away from the ranch. The soft tissue he bit into barely made it bleed versus frenzy even more, the thrashing of its front legs making its neck a riskier target.

It was when he released what his left paw was holding, in hopes of grabbing the animal's front legs, that the piglet's weight pulled his head down. With his fangs now holding tens of pounds, Alex growled as his free paw tried to grab its front legs. As soon as he did, the animal's free front hoof started smashing into and raking his arm, cutting his skin and ripping out his fur.

The pain was quick to intensify with each impact, Alex's eyes squinting and another growl sounding every time he felt a hit. *Son of a bitch.* He bit down harder after several before another few hits made him release its neck with a painful grunt. By then he was nearing the street he'd crossed to reach the ranch and could hear cheering and baseballs hitting steel bats. Once he was past that field, he was home free.

The sound of a vehicle coming made him stop just before he could see the road. As it passed, he tried again to grab both the piglet's front legs, only for the animal to hit his wrist, as well as his arm. The pain from the sharp edge of its hooves hitting an open wound caused Alex's grip to fail, and the piglet fell to the ground. It got several feet from him before he started after it, breaking through the line of brush at the edge of the road.

He looked to his left just in time to see a police cruiser coming his way, and backpedaled into the brush, his hind paws almost striking a felled branch. Several yards away his catch was fleeing into the night, squealing.

The sound of the cruiser slowing down near where he'd almost lost his balance pumped more adrenaline into his veins.

Chapter 12 – On The Hunt Again

Tuesday, October 11th, 2011
Moon Phase – Waxing Gibbous

Alex's breaths ran ragged for several seconds as he tried to focus and decide what to do. Moving south was the only option he saw. Anything else and he'd be just as screwed as staying still. After two steps in that direction, the sound of a door lock popping made him drop to all fours and slow his pace. His head kept turning back to watch for any lights hitting the brush beyond the cruiser's headlights.

Three, then five, then seven seconds passed with no hint of it, though Alex couldn't stop worrying about what the officer had seen. If they had seen him clearly enough. What they would report, even if they weren't sure. *Why the hell did I listen to him?* Alex thought as he slowed to a stop and spun around, dropping almost to his chest. The headlights, and the cruiser, had to be over thirty or more yards from him now. If he went too far south, he'd run out of shrubbery to hide around, and then the streetlights that were working would light him up.

After a glance left, Alex thought of breaking just his head through the brush to see what was there. The officer had yet to cross into the area, and he heard no footsteps against grass nearby. If they were still a good distance from him... Alex cut that thought off upon remembering the officer and canine unit at the ranch. He had to have called for backup, and if that meant a perimeter would be set up, he didn't have long.

The thought of being caught or pursued made the entirety of Alex's body tremble and stuck him in place. He took some breaths to try and calm down, the thought of his father hearing the backup call weighing his limbs down further.

It was as the seconds ticked by that he noticed the cruiser wasn't doing anything but idling. *He couldn't have seen me that well, not if he's just sitting there. Not if he was that far away with just the moon out.* A touch of warmth reached his gut at that, and he felt some of the weight lift from his limbs. Then it dawned on him: if the officer was inside the cruiser, they wouldn't hear his paws against the ground, and directly north was a channel that ran into the nearby drainage basin.

Alex was quick to act on that realization, trotting north as fast as he could go. When the noise of the idling engine crested, he slowed for a second to look around, resuming at full speed after he didn't see anything. Soon the treeline approached, and Alex again slowed his pace, halting at the very edge to scout out the area. The unhindered moonlight made everything he saw look spot-lit, the headlights of an oncoming car doing little to increase the brightness. Even so, he could see the basin just across the street.

Despite the growing feeling of being watched creeping over his skin, once he felt safe enough, he pushed off with his legs and didn't stop until he was at the creek that lead to his neighborhood park.

Along the way, he found traces of Shane's scent among the grasses and atop concrete, though none that led into the creek he was using. When Alex looked back, towards the basin and the skatepark beyond, the question of where Shane lived returned to mind. What he was supposed to do to make up for the loss of his catch quickly eclipsed it, though.

His first idea was to wait a while, then come back and see if he could find his prey. The police wouldn't spend all night combing the area, certainly not for one missing pig, but if he couldn't find it and came back empty-handed... *How late can I stay up?* With his heart and lungs at last relaxing, Alex felt much more fatigued versus anything resembling a desire to sleep.

It was nine-thirty when I left...must have been at least an hour since then. Unable to recall the last time he stayed up anywhere close to 2:00 a.m., two, three more hours at most was all that he believed he could manage.

He returned home to find the yard clean of fresh animal scents, and the time at 11:23, according to his desk clock. Near it was his phone, the screen showing no missed texts or calls. *Soon as midnight comes, I'm going back.* Alex then opened one of his windows, and the guest window, and starting from the front door, did a check of the outside from every available window. With the evening breezes still going south, the wooded area across the street was where he hoped he'd see something he could feed on.

For the first fifteen minutes of his pacing of the house, he ignored the rumbling of his stomach that had started before he came inside. When nothing presented itself within that same time, a glass of water and four hot dogs were what he made for a snack. Several yawns got away from him before he finished eating, pushing him to head back out early.

The sight of Bailey sleeping on his bed made him pause for a moment when he returned to his room. His pet's eyes were on him in a second, but his head stayed down, and no growls sounded from him. *Good boy, Bailey. I'll be home soon.* Once his bedroom window was shut, Alex left him be and was outside shortly after.

As he retraced his steps towards and along the creek he'd used, the yawning that had started at home progressed into longer and more frequent events. The sight of the basin, how much more land he had to cover before he could even start searching, caused it again and made him shake his head.

It was as he continued towards the bridge that something he hadn't considered came to him: if the stable near his high school had been cleared of animals, how many more months would it be before similar places in the area started shutting down or moving? The idea of traveling out of town every few months to reduce the likelihood was quick to follow, but so did a twinge of sadness that he didn't expect. Alex fought the uncomfortable feeling back as the bridge came into view. Having an excuse to get out of town, possibly spend some daylight hours roaming without fear of being seen, couldn't be that terrible of a thing.

Once he was underneath the bridge, the lack of police lights in the distance relieved a bit of his now-building exhaustion. The floodlights above the football and baseball fields were still on, which he expected, but as he came closer, he heard no more cheering. As he came within several yards of the street, Alex stuck close to the nearby building and, as soon as he could, he peered around its edge. Though the grass and trees obstructed much of his view, the cruiser from before was gone. He then let a minute pass, crossing the road only after no cars drove by and he heard nothing in line with footsteps.

The shallow recession by the road was where he started his search, his head pulling up every few seconds to watch for oncoming vehicles. The scent of the pig eluded him until he found a weak trace from it near where the cruiser stopped. How much road and area there was behind him made several possibilities of where it had gone come to mind, but if he was only now picking up its scent, and on the ground instead of the air... *Where the hell did it go?*

Alex moved north again, past a shallow depression and towards the concrete-lined channel that ran into to the basin. The sides went down at least a full story, and there was some water at the bottom, but no hint of the piglet. The possibility that it had fallen into the other side came to mind, but that was proven false ten seconds later. With everything to the north being industrial buildings and parking lots, all of which were illuminated, Alex questioned if the police, or someone else, had found it and taken it. For the next few minutes, he couldn't come up with a better explanation for why he'd not found its scent beyond a few spots in the grass, and after he went even further east, enough to let him see Industrial Boulevard once again, it became the only explanation that made sense.

Alex then groaned and covered his face, torn between wanting to kick himself for losing his catch after all that effort, and hoping another option presented itself before he couldn't stay up any longer. Another yawn escaped his lungs as he wracked his brain for ideas. Trying the ranch again came to mind, though he didn't have to go far to see that not only were the police still there, but the silver pick-up he'd seen a week before had joined them.

The shopping center he'd passed was his next idea, but even after minutes of pacing, no scents of living rodents came on the breezes. He then headed west again, back to his middle school. The baseball field was barren, and the only scents besides those from Shane that he found amongst the grass and concrete were from loose canines and felines. He shook his head and massaged his throat when the thought of attacking such animals surfaced. Further west, he darted across another street, towards an area he'd passed a month ago on his way to his high school. The scents of the stable animals were indeed gone, the lone scent that caught his interest leading him north into the shrubbery and trees, but to nothing he could chase and catch.

Alex then stopped to think some more, only to feel his eyelids, and his head, growing heavy. The sudden increase in his heart rate snapped him awake, but only for as long as it took him to once again reach the creek leading north. Another yawn got away as he closed his water-soaked eyes for even longer, and by the time he reached the park the creek ran by, he'd begun wiping his eyes.

With no one in sight, the park illuminated only by the moon, Alex diverted into the southernmost part of the park. Expecting at least one duck to be resting near the pond, he found none beyond their weakening scents in the grass. The wooded area near his house was the last place he checked. Two fresh scents were among the felled branches and leaves, but both led him towards, and then up, one of the many trees.

When he retreated to the safety of home, Alex didn't go straight to sleep. Instead, he popped open his window and kept watch. Something had to come around.

Five minutes later his eyelids closed, and exhaustion took over for a second. He shook himself awake, stopping shy of slapping himself, but after another few minutes the same thing happened, this time as he watched from the bay window. His breathing was slowing along with his heartrate, something he tried to counter to no lasting effect.

I can't fall asleep now. Alex told himself that for another few minutes, and got in another quarter of an hour of observing before his upright stance, as well as his all-fours stance, started getting wobbly.

Alex felt little besides defeat as he headed back to his room, anchoring one leg atop his bed to counter what he'd just felt. His eyelids drooped again within seconds, and five minutes later, at 2:05 a.m., he couldn't keep himself up any longer. After he flopped onto his bed and settled, sleep took over within a minute.

Wednesday, October 12th, 2011
Moon Phase – Full

When he awoke the next morning to the sun streaming past his blinds, his desk clock was the first thing he looked towards.

9:31 a.m.

No. Oh, no. Alex's throat immediately tensed, and his left paw curled into a fist as he swore repeatedly to himself. Already he was hungry for something, but it wouldn't be dim outside until 6:00 p.m. or so. *I can last that long. I won't go feral like this.*

When he at last got up and approached the hallway, his father's scent was quick to reach his nostrils. A brief snore was all he needed to know he was home, with a check of his phone showing no missed messages or voicemails. Even so, Alex couldn't shake the feeling he'd gotten word of what happened last night, or that his father would start questioning him as soon as he saw him.

When his stomach began rumbling a minute later, the thought of eating anything and finding out the hunger was already affecting him made his arms wrap around his chest to counter an under-pelt shiver. If his parents could leave him alone for the day...but that still left Bailey. Alex settled on keeping him outside with his dishes, the garage door open for him to cool off in if he needed it.

Another half hour of his stomach grumbling passed before he found a glass and got some water. How good the snacks in the cupboard smelled when he came close made his hunger feel more self-imposed than unwanted and the hot dogs he'd not eaten came to mind, causing a lick of his fangs.

When he pulled them from the fridge, only one was cooked; within four bites, he could feel the twinge in his stomach that told him the other hunger was affecting him. He swore silently several times, regret and fear flooding his head for a while after.

He eventually left the kitchen with a fresh glass of water, and once his bedroom window was open, he found a book to read and tried to get absorbed in it. The sound of his father rousing snapped him away from it a while later, and as Alex listened to him get ready for the day, his gaze kept shifting between the book and his bedroom door, what he planned to say staying in mind and ready.

When his father did appear, dressed in half of his police uniform, the recoil through his body didn't evade Alex's attention. "Hey, Dad," he said when he was met with silence.

"What happened last night, Son?"

The lack of extreme emotions in his father's tone relaxed Alex's nerves a touch. He had to be talking about the disturbance call. "I wanted to get something early, to be ready for that hunger."

"From the calls I got, it sounded like you weren't alone." Alex cursed Shane for being so reckless. "Was it the one you told us about?"

"Yeah."

"Why were you there with him?"

"Because he followed me. Said I had the same idea he did."

"So, the missing pigs?"

Alex nodded. "About that, though..." He felt his ears start to bend back. "I lost the one I caught."

His father sighed and laid his head against one palm.

"I tried to find it. Had no luck."

"Because we found it," his father replied after his hand was pulled away.

Thought so.

"So, because that happened, what now?"

An unconscious swallow came when Alex didn't speak for two seconds. The idea of killing someone's pet remained as morbid and gut-wrenching as before.

"Alex?"

"I'll have to suck it up until night comes again."

"So it's already affecting you? That hunger?"

Alex nodded.

"Oh, my God." His father's tone, and the sight of him planting his face into his palm, slammed a dagger of guilt into Alex's heart.

For a while neither of them spoke, giving Alex enough time to notice his father's scent. His brain and stomach were already giving it a pleasant edge.

"And you've never dealt with this before?" his father eventually asked.

"The first time I did." Alex responded. "I stayed hungry for hours until night came." His father didn't reply. "I'll manage. I did before."

His father hummed in response.

"What happened to the pig?"

"The owner took it to be put down after one of the officers found it."

Figures.

"Regardless though, don't go back there. I don't think the officers who reported to me and dispatch really saw you, but after what you and this guy did there, there will be some kind of surveillance of that area."

Alex glanced at his father again. He wanted to respond with, "I'll try", since the place was still one where he could get something if he had no other choice. "Alright."

His father then stepped away from the door, towards the kitchen. Alex gave him a few seconds, then got up and headed outside through his parent's room. The backyard was barren, as usual, and no noteworthy noises had sounded for the last hour. With the garage door key in his paw, he slid the bedroom door open and made for the garage, slipping inside once it was unlocked. The sight of the unused cooler became a cruel reminder of the night before as he checked the latches on the rolling door. All he had to do now was lure Bailey out after his father left, and then keep to himself until nightfall.

By 10:30 a.m. the hunger was picking up strength and Alex had retreated to his room, the door shut to prevent both Bailey coming in and more of his father's scent from reaching him. And despite his attempts to distract himself from it, his heartbeat was remaining elevated. *Keep it together. I've done this before*, Alex thought as he tried to read one of his novels.

The hunger was noticeably worse after another hour passed. Paying any attention to a book or similar thing became a trial as the void in his stomach intensified. How dry his throat started feeling around noon provided the sole counter to his fears of treating his father's scent like that of a potential meal, and he made for the kitchen.

"Everything okay, Son?" his father asked when he heard his claws clicking on the tile.

"Yeah," Alex replied as he refilled his glass.

"Then, about tonight, have you thought about where you'll go?"

Figuring his father knew about the evacuation of the animals at his high school, Alex answered as best he could. "There's an animal farm near Marcus's neighborhood."

"That's quite a way north."

"I know. Just an idea," Alex said as he found some straws and took a drink.

"Anyplace else?"

"Uh, I guess the parks and ponds around here."

"That's a little vague."

"I mean the park down the road, and the pond near Nathan's place."

His father took a few seconds. "And what if none of those work out?"

Alex sighed quietly as his stomach began to rumble. The ranch was his best bet in that case, and for a moment, he felt like his father knew it. "Then I'll have to take what I can get. Like before." When his father didn't respond, Alex returned to his room, this time powering on his XBOX and hoping a game would be more effective at distracting from his hunger.

For a while, it was; the rumbling of his abdomen and spreading emptiness through his muscles started winning back his attention just before 1:00 p.m. With the game paused, Alex leaned against the head of his bed and laid a paw over his stomach. Five more hours of this, and likely worse? He gave himself a few minutes without distractions before turning his console off. He couldn't imagine the hunger crippling him in any way, but he'd yet to go more than five hours without dealing with it.

When Alex forced himself to breathe slower, in the hopes of calming down, his heart didn't cooperate. The knocking on his door a while later only made it speed up. Once he was settled in his desk chair, he pulled his paw away from his abdomen.

"Hey, Dad," he said once the door opened and his father walked in. His skeptical expression, and the stall in his response, left Alex hoping he at least looked calm.

"Something wrong?"

Alex shook his head. "No. Just thinking about taking a nap."

"When you're hungry?"

"I've got to kill time somehow."

His father paused again. "Alright. I'll see you tomorrow then, Son."

Alex nodded in response. "You too, Dad." His father then began to close his door, and until he heard his truck start up, Alex stayed seated.

The scent-trail his father had left relaxed his stomach and made his tongue twitch, getting him to move faster towards the kitchen pantry. After a few seconds, he found the dog treats he'd bought for Bailey and poured three into his paw. The scents coming off them were more pleasing than he expected, but with getting his dog outside a sudden priority, once he found him resting on the office sofa, he wasted no time saying his name and showing him the treats.

Bailey's expression remained blank, and his tail didn't move, even as Alex came closer. Certain he was torn on what to think, Alex tossed one of the treats at him. His pet still didn't move, opting to simply crane his neck to reach and snap up the treat, once it stopped bouncing.

"C'mon, Bailey. With me," Alex said as he walked away. After five seconds without hint of his pet, he returned to the office. "Outside, boy." This time, Alex returned to his room and waited, leaving his door and the one into his parents' bedroom open. Several minutes went by with no sign of Bailey taking interest, and he set the treats aside.

As he started thinking about other ways to get him outside, the sound of creaking and claws on wood reached him through his open window. Alex's head snapped towards it and he came in close before questioning what was entering his yard. A cat was the first thing he thought of, his head shaking again as the thought of using one for food entered his head.

As he continued to stare in the direction he thought the noise had come from, from behind the garage, he saw an upright, black and tan-furred werewolf emerge. Shane turned his direction as his flesh began to chill, the sight of a slab of meat in his right paw the only thing keeping Alex from recoiling in horror.

Chapter 13 – An Unexpected Guest

Wednesday, October 12th, 2011
Moon Phase – Full

Shane wasted not a second before closing in on Alex's bedroom window. As he did, the part of Alex's brain that was running wild with questions, the part of him that was making him quake about Shane being right outside his home, was losing ground to how much of a relief the meat he was holding would be.

Alex leaned back as Shane came within ten feet of the window. His muzzle showed no hint of viciousness, but what he demanded was delivered with some concern in his tone. "Let me in."

The scents from the meat relaxed Alex's stomach, slowing his response and making Shane's lips curl. "You're...kidding me."

"You're hungry. I knew it would happen."

"You insisted. One each."

"And you lost yours. Wasn't my doing." Alex missed his window to respond, being left wondering how Shane knew that. "I'm not playing games with you. Let me in, and I'll hand this over. If that's too much to ask, then I'm keeping it."

Alex swallowed as the meat scents continued to taunt his stomach and brain. He couldn't. Who was this guy to demand that he do anything of the sort? But then, his hunger was still building. If he let it get too severe... How much would he be letting this guy learn about himself and his family by letting him in? "The garage is open. Use that."

Shane was shaking his head before Alex finished. "You let me in, you'll get fed, and then I'm gone come sundown."

"You came all this way in broad daylight, though."

"Because I know what I'm doing. And be thankful that I did; you don't want that hunger pushing you to kill your dog, or someone else."

Alex looked away from Shane as those thoughts went through his head, the sound of paws on carpet making him turn fully around. Bailey was standing at the door, his tail still but his attention fixed on the window.

When Alex closed his eyes before a lengthy exhale, Shane continued. "That other room. Is it empty?"

"Yeah," Alex said after looking at him again.

"Then that's all I need. You don't want me bothering you or going anywhere else inside, fine."

Alex swallowed again. Four hours of him around, in exchange for being fed and sating his hunger. Would Shane really leave him to suffer if he refused? And his mother would be home before nightfall. What if she saw him? Those concerns and questions, and more, turned over and over for the next minute.

"Behind the house," Alex at last said. "Use the window."

"Fine by me." Shane stepped away when he finished speaking.

As he did, Alex rushed to close the door to his parents' bedroom, and then his. Bailey recoiled into the hallway and tucked his tail from how quick Alex had moved, but stayed silent. When Shane was at the window, despite the part of Alex's brain screaming that this was a bad idea, he picked at the window until he could get a hold of it and let him in.

As soon as Shane had both hind paws on the carpet, he thrust the meat into Alex's chest. His body was trembling from what he'd just done, and his ears were laid flat as well, even once the meat was in his hands.

"Like I said," Shane began, "I won't go anywhere if it bothers you that much." He then sat down on the futon in front of the window, his eyes glancing around at the books on the wall opposite.

Alex let out a few more shaky breaths before turning his attention to the meat. The slab was easily half the weight of the pig he'd lost, all of which looked edible to his stomach. It was tense yet moist where his paws held it, though whatever warmth the meat once housed was fading.

Where Shane had gotten a slab like this was put aside as soon as Alex's first bite was taken. He tore pieces from it every few seconds, each one filling the pit of his stomach. Between his first few bites, Alex's attention stayed on Shane. Only once did he look away from the bookshelves, up at him. Nothing about his face or muzzle was in line with an emotion to be cautious of, but his animalistic stare wasn't calming either.

When his mother came back to mind, Alex looked towards the closet. If the door to the room was closed, his mother would likely avoid it…but if she didn't, she'd find Shane. That concern raised another: had his father told his mother about the hunger, about what he said he needed to do? Alex saw no reason to think he hadn't, and if that was so, he had to leave the house at sundown too.

"My folks will be home before you leave," Alex said after licking his teeth and muzzle.

"I figured," Shane said before he looked aside. "You thinking of hiding me in there?"

"It's big enough."

Shane took a second before responding, his muzzle curling the longer he took. "I hate cramped spaces, but whatever. If you think it'll work."

"It will," Alex said before he bit off another chunk of the slab. He held off on telling Shane any more than that, and when his stomach was at last filled, what was left of the slab was little more than one mouthful. Though relieved that his hunger was gone, when he next looked at Shane, Alex found saying even just 'thanks' difficult.

Shane noticed his reluctance when he finally got it out, and his response was delayed. "If you really want to thank me, make sure what you catch from now on doesn't have a chance to get away from you."

"I'll do that," Alex said. After his attention returned to what remained of the slab, the dry feeling of his throat got him to leave the room. Once out in the hallway, the question of where Shane had gotten that meat returned. He couldn't have killed something for it; the piece had been too clean-cut, as though a butcher had cut it. Did he know someone who was able to get him the animals he needed? If he did, why had he killed so many a month before?

Several more questions went through Alex's head as he freed his paws from holding the sliver of meat, and then filled a glass with some water and ice. There were still three and a half hours or so until Shane left, and as he sipped his drink, Alex considered questioning him. He had plenty of time to do it, but outside of simple stuff, he couldn't see Shane doing anything more than blowing him off or, at best, feeding him a line.

Might as well get him some water. When he returned to the guest bedroom, Alex found Shane resting his head on his propped arms and paws. The sight pulled Catherine's remark, about him looking like a sleepy dog, out of memory, getting his lips to raise into a canine smile before Shane opened one eye, and then the other.

Alex lifted the second glass a bit when he was certain Shane's attention was on him, and then set it on the nearby table. "Read one if you're bored," he said after tossing his head to the left.

"Not my kinds of books," Shane said.

"I'm guessing reading is mostly what you do on these days."

"Until night comes."

Alex weighed his next words for a second. "So how did you get here? The creek, or that lot across the way?"

"I wasn't seen, if that's what you're getting at."

"In the middle of the day?"

Shane exhaled noticeably. "I'm guessing you think every window, house, car and the like is something to be worried about." Alex stalled on answering. "If that's even a bit true, you're too paranoid."

"Then you've not noticed the increase in police patrolling around here."

"Different issue, and yes I have."

"So, you traveled at least three blocks, meat in one hand, and no one saw you?"

Shane's response came after a second. "Yes, and don't think I'm telling you where I live."

"You know where I live, and you're in my house."

"In exchange for what you needed to not turn on your dog, or your family, and use them as something to feed on." That response locked Alex's throat. "I'm not here trying to get something out of you, but I wasn't lying when I said I'm keeping an eye on you. I could hear that pig squealing as soon as you lost it, and I knew what that meant."

"And so you killed another animal, or what?" Alex replied, hoping Shane would take the bait.

"Just be thankful you got fed, and that what you were feeling didn't get any worse."

With Shane's answer, the places where Alex had found his scent returned to mind. If he really was that certain about traveling the streets in broad daylight, the areas south and east of the skatepark, places he knew were packed with houses, were where he likely lived. And whatever direction or location he'd come from, he would leave a trail on his way back.

"Somehow I doubt you would've left me alone if I refused."

A guttural growl sounded from Shane a second later, locking Alex's attention onto him. His fangs were fully exposed, and his fur stood on end. "Don't you fucking dare act like that was something you were willing to ignore."

Alex's ears folded back and his head lowered some as Shane half spoke, half growled at him. It took him ceasing to growl, plus a few seconds more, for Alex to recover his courage. "I wasn't... That wasn't my idea."

"Waiting until the sun went down was your idea, wasn't it?" Alex didn't answer. "I don't care how tough or careful you think you are, you would've been just as willing to feed on human flesh by that point."

The injection of anger, disgust, and---what sounded like---fear into Shane's tone sapped Alex's urge to ask how he was so certain of that, although now he couldn't help wondering if he'd lived through that, and if so, when.

"No, I wasn't about to leave you alone. Because I didn't want to hear that you'd murdered and eaten someone. And talk tough all you want, you would've accepted that meat at some point."

Alex sighed as his eye-contact with Shane broke; the noise came out layered with a growl. Any response he could think to give for the next few minutes was tossed aside out of worry of pissing Shane off again, or simply said in his head. For the same length of time, he didn't budge from where he stood, until the sound of Bailey's paws against the carpet reached him.

His pet came to a stop in the hallway, several feet from the door. When Alex checked on him, his attention shifted between him and a scent near the floor, which he was certain was Shane's. "You want out, boy?" His pet glanced at him before taking in more of the scent. With Shane so close, the thought of opening the door to his parent's room, of allowing his 'guest' access to their scents, was countered with speculation about why Bailey had come. Had it been the raised voices, or was he looking to get into his room? Both felt plausible, and Shane had already approached him with that room's windows open, but his pet stayed at his current distance once Alex opened his bedroom door.

Alex glanced at Shane again, and his eyes shifted to meet his. Though he said nothing, his stare remained just as piercing, and Alex soon left the room in favor of his own. This time, Bailey followed him and laid down on his doggy bed. *Good boy.*

The house remained quiet until Alex heard Shane lapping the water from the glass he'd left him, a stretch of almost an hour. He set the novel he was reading aside and inched past Bailey to find Shane leaning over the glass, his paws cupped around the rim to catch the water that sloshed from his muzzle between each lap. When Shane noticed his presence, he stopped. "Never thought of that," was how Alex responded, and Shane went back to drinking. As soon as he was done, he sat back down.

The urge to question Shane inched its way back as Alex stood in the doorway. He had to have calmed down by now. After picking up the glass, which was currently half-drunk and missing the straws, "Uh…" was all he managed instead of a full question.

"What?" Shane's tone held no extremes.

"About this animal hunger…"

Shane sighed out of his nostrils and shook his head before Alex finished. "I'm not giving you any excuse to think you can fight that."

"I can handle it for a few hours."

"And that's all you deserve to know if you were about to let it claw at your guts all day."

"Then was I supposed to hunt in broad daylight, to risk being seen, chased and shot at?"

"No, you were supposed to kill what you caught, not let it get away. You'll always have a night to hunt, and a month to prepare. You screwed up the first part, and if I hadn't come, you would've killed someone."

Before Alex realized it, he'd blurted out, "And how would you know that?" The temperature of his skin fell a few degrees, and stayed that way as Shane locked his gaze onto him again.

"Because the first time I made that mistake," Shane began, his voice becoming more growl-laced with each word, "someone I cared for smelled like an easy meal."

Alex's thoughts returned to his parents. To how easily his stomach relaxed when he'd caught their scents while hungry. Some of his distress resurfaced, clogging his throat.

"No, I didn't kill them. Because that scared the shit out of me, and I kept away from them until I found something I could kill. No, I don't know what will happen if that 'animal hunger' builds for as long as you were about to let it. Because I'm not about to risk finding out, and if you're smart, you won't either."

Shane went quiet after that, and though Alex didn't want him to have the last word twice in a row, speaking now would give away that something had gotten to him. Hoping refilling their glasses would give him the time to clear his throat, he did just that, with a few easy breaths removing most of the tension.

After a final swallow, he returned to the room. "I'm not trying to piss you off, you understand," Alex said after setting the second glass down.

"Then whatever beef you have with me, stop letting it lead your head and tongue."

"You say that like it was and still is in my best interest to be kept in the dark," Alex replied, trying not to sound agitated himself.

"As far as I can see, you put the pieces together and didn't make stupid mistakes that destroyed your livelihood."

"So, it was out of the question to say even one thing to me? Even a warning that I'd be hungry for animal meat?"

This time, Shane took a second to answer. "I'll give you that."

No shit you should.

"But what's done is done. You know what to expect now, and you know what I don't want to do, so how about we leave it at that?"

An urge to snap back at Shane hung in Alex's head at that response, until he closed his eyes and exhaled out his muzzle. He couldn't see himself getting any further with this guy, at least for right now. Refusing to answer him on that front, he checked on the closet. "If you hear a deadbolt unlock, or my dog run for the front door, get inside."

"And when the coast is clear?"

Alex shut the closet door, and then tapped it with two digits.

"Works for me. Do it after six-fifteen."

The next hour went by with neither Alex nor Shane speaking to each other. The sound of water being lapped only briefly got Alex's attention away from the novel in his paws, the arrival of 5:00 p.m. getting him to listen for the sound of the front door unlocking.

When he heard what he thought were tires on pavement, he set the book aside, his pulse rising a few beats. At the same time, he began fretting about what his mother was expecting. If his father had mentioned the hunger to her...

The remaining sliver of meat then returned to mind. Hoping his mother wasn't outside, Alex hurried to retrieve it from the kitchen, his quickened steps against the carpet drawing no response from Shane. Once it was on a fresh paper plate and in his paws, Alex didn't wait for a hint of the front door deadbolt unlocking, though it wasn't long before it became clear he'd panicked.

Around 5:40 p.m. he heard similar noises, these ones coming further up the driveway, and then the clicking he was waiting for sounded. Before Alex moved, he heard Shane get up and slip into the closet, closing the door behind him. After Bailey rushed off for the front door, Alex followed Shane, leaving his bedroom door open and closing the guest room door behind him. With his heart already racing, he went over what to tell his mother as he heard her come inside, speak sweetly to Bailey, and then lead him back towards her room.

"It's okay," she said after Bailey's paws stopped impacting the carpet a distance from her door. "Alex?"

"In here," Alex responded, faking a weakened tone.

"Are you okay?"

"I will be." He then heard his mother walk past the door, open her bedroom door, and then call for Bailey. When he didn't budge, she led him outside through the front door instead.

She returned to the hallway afterward, and then stopped by the door. "Can I come in?"

For a moment, Alex wanted to allow it. "No. I'll be fine."

"What's wrong?"

Oh, boy. His mother's responses felt in line with being told he'd be hungry. "Couldn't catch anything. Stomach feels like it's collapsing." His mother didn't respond. He pictured her putting her hands over her mouth, edging closer to tears. "Keep inside tonight. I'll be alright."

"Why?"

Alex breathed out slowly, hoping his mother would hear. "Just concerns. Stay inside."

He was met with silence again, but when his mother spoke up, he heard the hints of her holding back some emotions. "Alright."

Alex released his caught breath only when he was certain his mother had left the hallway, and even then, he released it with no audio. Feeling like all he'd done was give cause for his parents to question his behavior, he sat against the door and watched the outside as the sun continued to set.

As he did so, his ears stayed alert for any footsteps nearby. For the moment his mother was staying on the northern end of the house, around the kitchen and living room. She only went into her room once, and just to use the bathroom. Bailey meanwhile had headed back into his bedroom after sniffing at the underside of the guest room door.

With no idea how much time had passed since Shane had started hiding, when he felt it was dark enough, he listened one last time for anything nearby, and when he was ready, got up, slid the window open, and waited for the air conditioner to start up.

He tapped the door as soon as it did and stood back. Shane was quick to slip out, keeping the door from making a sound as it opened, and gave him a look after checking the room. "You're not following me," he said, his voice just louder than the whir of the fan blades.

"You stay here, you'll get caught, and then we're both screwed." Shane looked aside at the window, and then back at him. "That what you want?" Alex then glanced at the room's door. "Then keep standing there."

Shane let out a frustrated huff in response. Alex curled his lips and muzzle as if to snarl back at him, to at least look aggressive. When Shane at last started moving, after several seconds of unflinching staring, Alex relaxed his jaws, and then waited for the sound of him jumping the fence again. Within five seconds, he was over.

Alex gave him until the fan blades stopped whirring, which felt like a couple minutes, before leaving the house himself, the sliver of meat held in one paw. Right away he found Shane's trail, but opted to leave through the side gate instead, slipping under the bay window as he went.

I'm sorry, Mom. Shane's trail had run under the window as well, and into the wooded area across the street. Alex followed it as far as he was comfortable with, which was enough to tell Shane had taken a route south that ran behind two rows of houses. *So that's the route he took.*

With that knowledge in mind, Alex found a spot far back in the mass of brush and trees, the meat at the ready to eat or toss away.

Chapter 14 – Prelude To A Search

Wednesday, October 12th, 2011
Moon Phase – Full

I shifted at eight-forty in the morning yesterday... Better not spend more than an hour and a half out here. As Alex tried to recreate Shane's route in his head, something began to dampen his drive to track him down. If he found where Shane lived, what would be the outcome, or the benefit? He'd been little more than evasive or agitated in response to his questions, and Alex couldn't see him being willing to share his source of meat.

But then, he was in the dark about a lot of things related to Shane. Locating his home would finally lessen how much of an upper hand he had. When his thoughts returned to the incident from the week before, Shane's words gave him a moment's pause. Was he really watching him? Outside of the marked tree, he'd found no reason to believe so.

How snippy he'd been all day only furthered Alex's doubts. Eventually, he could see no explanation besides Shane speaking in anger instead of sincerity. *Better keep an eye on the lot for a while regardless.*

* * *

After what felt like an hour had passed, Alex headed back across the street. When the air-conditioner started up again, he picked at the window and got himself back inside. The guest room door was still closed, but with an ear near it, he could hear something from the television in the living room. Figuring his mother was sitting where she could see him open the door, he took a breath, gripped the doorknob and, hoping his fib from before had worked, twisted it before inching the door open.

His assumption was proven right. His mother was sitting on the left side of the couch, Bailey lying in her lap. As soon as she saw him, the TV was turned off.

"Hey, Mom," Alex said before he stepped into the hallway, the half-full glass for Shane held in one paw.

"Did you---" She cut herself off.

"Yeah, I'm fine," Alex said as he came closer, trying not to look pleased. "Didn't mean to scare you."

She shook her head. "You didn't. I just..."

Despite no further words, the gut punch Alex felt from his mother getting upset kept him from leaving the room, or looking directly at her for more than a second. With Bailey's attention not wavering from his massive wolf-man form, Alex didn't try to approach her, as much as he wanted to.

A peek into the kitchen revealed 7:43 p.m. as the time. "I'll change back in about an hour," Alex eventually said. "It shouldn't wake you up."

His mother sniffled. "Don't worry about that. I'm just glad you're okay."

"Me too," Alex said. His mother didn't respond, and his building thirst urged him into the kitchen. Shaking away the urge he felt to sniff at the glass in his paw, Alex filled another one and returned to his room.

Eventually he heard his mother coax Bailey off her lap, and then after a few minutes, she started heading his direction. His room light was left off when she peered in, allowing his night-vision to reveal how much she'd calmed down. "I'll see you tomorrow," she said after a second.

With his glass set aside, Alex got up from his chair and came closer. Though the inch back his mother took didn't escape his notice, he laid a paw on her shoulder before responding. "You too. Love you." His mother, in turn, reached up to hold, then pat and rub his paw and arm until she was ready to depart for her room.

* * *

Until he felt his pulse increase and his fingers go numb, Alex stayed occupied with a pair of magazines. The loss of his claws came first, then when he was in the pantry and down on the floor, he began hearing cracks from the bones in his muzzle and hind legs. Once they reshaped, his muscles structure followed, as did his tail and ears. All that remained then was his chest and ribs, and every pop of bone and shrinking of muscle allowed less air into his lungs to assist with his increased heartbeat.

Eventually the last part of his skeleton was set, and it was over. He was human again.

As Alex rubbed what remained of his pelt off his skin, exposing it to the cold of the house again, he heard Bailey approaching the pantry doors and let him in. His pet's muzzle went straight for his face but stopped short of licking him in favor of sniffing him, his breaths blowing away leftover strands of fur before causing him to sneeze.

"I know, boy," Alex replied after a short chuckle. He rubbed Bailey's head once one of his arms was free of shed fur, and this time, his pet licked him.

Thursday, October 13th, 2011
Moon Phase – Waning Gibbous
6:53 a.m.

When he woke the next morning, he found Bailey sleeping back to back to him. His pet was roused at the first movement he made, though a belly rub kept him from getting up. As his parents began to rouse as well, Alex slipped out of bed and got dressed, his XBOX helping pass the time until his mother emerged from her bedroom.

"Morning," Alex said as she stood in the doorway.

"You sore at all?"

Alex shook his head. "Not really." His mother didn't respond, or move from where she stood, and after a moment, he got up and gave her a hug. The hold she had on him strengthened within a second, a hint that she was as happy as Bailey to see him as a human again.

When his mother at last loosened her hold, she spoke. "About yesterday, why was your stomach hurting?"

Alex took a second to think. "It wasn't hurting. I was just really hungry."

"For how long?"

"Quite a while. That was my fault."

"How come?"

"The animal I caught that night. I lost it. Couldn't find it afterward." His mother's hold tightened again.

"Then, was that all you did that day? Sit in that room?"

Alex exhaled out his nose. "I didn't know what to expect. When it got bad, that was the best option I could see."

His mother didn't reply until her hold relaxed again. "Well, you're okay. That's what matters."

"Thanks, Mom," Alex said before she let go of him completely.

* * *

As he prepared to leave for class later that morning, the sound of his father getting ready for his day pushed a question into Alex's mind: had anything changed since yesterday? What he might have to do if hunting within the city became too risky followed, and stayed in mind as his father left his bedroom.

"Morning," Alex said when he saw him.

"Did everything work out?" his father asked, his tone not hinting at anything untoward.

Alex nodded in response. "Yeah. Stomach was driving me nuts, though."

"So, what was it you killed?"

How direct that question was made Alex shiver. His fib was delayed in turn. "A stray, I think. A large breed."

"You think?"

"There was no collar."

His father sighed, and Alex turned his head. Better this than letting him know he'd let Shane in the house, meat offering or not.

"I'm sorry, Dad. I didn't want to."

"How bad was it?" his father asked after a few seconds.

At first confused, after a glance at his abdomen, Alex answered. "Like I was going several days without food."

After his father's eyebrows rose, he spoke. "You're kidding me."

Alex shook his head, now feeling his pulse speed up. "I didn't know it would get that bad that fast."

His father took a long breath in response, one hand over his mouth. A cold fear gripped Alex's heart in turn.

"There was nothing else around?"

Alex shook his head again. "I wasn't seen, though."

"Regardless, that could've been someone's pet."

"I know, and I didn't want to, but it was starting to scare me, that hunger." A tightening of his jaw muscles followed Alex's response.

"Then I take it you have some ideas about how to avoid that next month?"

This time, Alex nodded. "A few."

"Then you and me and your mother can talk about them come Friday. What you two did the other night is getting the precinct to bring in more canine units, and from what I've been told, more patrols at night as well."

Great. Just fucking great. As soon as his father left him alone, Alex made up his mind on hunting down Shane, and as his classes that day went by, he thought over where to search, as well as when. He had a shift until seven after class, as well as Friday, but Saturday was completely open.

He gave his options a little thought before deciding to hold off the search until the weekend. He'd have more time then, and if he found where Shane lived after a few days' wait, he'd probably be less likely to think he tracked him down just because of the meat. Otherwise, if he found nothing, he'd eliminate however much of his neighborhood he could cover.

With Shane not showing his face throughout his five-hour shift, Alex returned home to Bailey's playful bounding and barks, and what remained of the meal his mother had fixed. One full plate was all he had before some playtime with his dog brought the time close to 7:45 p.m.

As he passed through the living room with his helmet and skateboard in hand, his mother spoke up, asking where he was going. "To the skatepark for a bit," Alex said.

"Isn't there a curfew in place?"

Alex stopped at the front door when he heard that. He'd completely forgotten, and after a second, said so in response.

Friday, October 14th, 2011
Moon Phase – Waning Gibbous

Throughout his classes and their respective tests the next day, the coming talk with his parents stayed in the back of Alex's mind. He'd already decided on what to tell them, leaving how things could go to weigh on him.

When Nathan rejoined him after the second class and asked how things had gone, Alex's tone betrayed his answer.

"Did something happen?"

Alex sighed, now feeling embarrassment creeping into his skin. "Yeah. I caught something, a small pig, but then it got away from me."

"Oh. So, you had to chase after it?"

Alex shook his head. "No, I had to run, from the police." His friend's eyes widened at that. "Yeah. The whole night was a waste."

Nathan covered his mouth and wrapped one arm around his chest before he responded. "Sorry to hear that, man." He then removed the hand from in front of his mouth. "You found something after that though, right?"

Seeing no benefit to mentioning Shane, and this time the dog he'd fibbed about that morning, Alex gave a quick answer. "Yeah, I did. Had to watch for patrols and hints of canine units the whole time, though. Never been that scared in my life."

"I'd imagine."

Though he felt an urge to add more, Alex refrained, and a few minutes later, he and Nathan parted ways with a handshake. For the length of his five-hour shift, he kept in mind what he planned to tell his folks. One or two ideas felt sufficient, if he explained himself well enough, or if they had no qualms about anything.

Even so, opening the front door once he was home, despite the scents of fresh lasagna leaking past it, made him tenser than he was comfortable with. Bailey's presence helped some, even once he was seated at the dinner table. By then, the tension had spread into his chest.

"Is something wrong?" his mother asked after a minute of silence.

Alex shook his head. "No. Just thinking."

"C'mon, Son. What's bothering you?"

Alex gave his father a glance at that and tried to breathe easy. For the moment, he had no answer that felt right and stayed silent.

When he did speak, it came after a few rubs of Bailey's head. "Next month, mostly."

"You said you had some ideas about that."

"A few, yeah." His parents gave him a moment, but in that moment, doubt about one of his ideas crept in. "I could go out of town to find something."

"Out of town?" His mother glanced aside and met his father's eyes.

"I think that's too drastic, Son. Plus, how would you stay hidden or eat while you're like that?"

"And what if something happened to you?"

"That too. We wouldn't know."

"I know," Alex said after a second. "Just an idea." The doubt he felt before delayed his next words. "I did come up with another one, but...it's not feasible, and I don't want to do it."

"How come?" his mother asked.

"Because I couldn't afford to buy an animal every month, and then have them go missing right after." As that sentence left his mouth, Alex noticed his father look away from him, and hoped he wouldn't bring up the dog he'd 'killed'.

His mother covered her mouth, aware of what he was implying. "Would you really do that?"

After an unconscious swallow was triggered in Alex's throat, and his silence went on for several seconds, his father spoke. "He already has."

"What?"

Damn it, Dad. Alex thought as his eyes shut and squinched. A shock of embarrassed and horrified cold hit his nerves at the same time, sealing his lips over his teeth as his head lowered.

Even though he couldn't see, he felt the attention of his parents pierce his skin and encourage him to slink back. "I didn't want to."

"But, why did you?" The disturbed tone from his mother was all too obvious, and in response, what Shane had told him sat in Alex's head.

He knew it was true, but saw nothing good coming from saying so. And he'd only screwed up once. He could keep from doing it again. He just had to be ready, or account for fatigue if he couldn't find anything.

"Alex?" his father prompted, and his spine went cold again.

"I was getting scared. I didn't know what would happen if that hunger lasted any longer, and just went with what I found."

"How long had it lasted by then?"

"More than ten hours," Alex said after doing a little math.

"He told me it felt like he'd gone a few days without food by then," his father said when his mother didn't comment, though the details clearly worried her. "That aside, are those all the ideas you had?"

"Yeah, I couldn't think of any more."

His father exhaled before continuing. "How many days until you change again?"

"Twenty-six."

"Then for now, keep thinking of ideas."

"Alright." After reopening his eyes, Alex glanced up at his parents. Convincing them that he would be safe, despite the heightened police presence and canine units, was an option, but not one he could see working beyond one more month. The idea of asking Shane who got him that meat then sprang to mind, before Alex questioned how willing he would be to say anything.

Alex tucked that thought away as the night went on. He had to find Shane first, and tomorrow he'd have all day to look.

Chapter 15 – Werewolf Scouting

Saturday, October 15th, 2011
Moon Phase – Waning Gibbous

It was nearing 11:00 a.m. when Alex left the house, his skateboard strapped to his snack-and-water-filled backpack, and with Bailey in tow. With the wind blowing southwest, the houses directly south of the skatepark were his first choice to check, and within half an hour, both he and his pet reached the street north of them.

Before they crossed, Alex offered Bailey some water from his cupped hand; his pet lapped up the entirety of a bottle before stopping, and once they were across, Alex turned into the first street they came to. Numerous foreign scents from outside and inside the houses reached his nose as they walked the length of the street. Of those, the weakest ones were what he tried to focus on, but despite that, none of the scents along the first street matched any of Shane's.

At the next street, Alex walked into a scent that made him slow his pace, but only for a second. Bailey however recognized the canine pheromones, and almost reversed their direction. "C'mon, boy. No," Alex said as he pulled at the leash. At the same time, he noticed an open window on the house he passed. *Great. We'll be smelling that for a while.*

The scent weakened some on the next street, though Bailey was quick to distract and keep his nose in the air when they walked into it. How easily it drew Alex's attention despite him trying to focus on other things made him shiver before he pinched his nose shut. When he released it after moving east one lot, the scent was still strong enough to cloud his head and nostrils; only when he reached the corner of the street did the scent weaken enough for others to stand out, and for Bailey to no longer be distracted by it.

For the next minute, as he questioned what to do in the face of the scent's strength, Alex knelt and stroked Bailey's pelt. Waiting for the winds to change direction would take too long, and possibly wouldn't help, so he soon decided on walking straight to the southmost street then---if the scent wasn't too distracting at that distance---start working his way north. Halfway down the second street, that very thing happened and he turned back, stopping at the end of the street.

Okay. Now what? With Bailey lolling his tongue and panting, Alex offered him another drink, then had one himself once his pet had finished. The intersection north of their location led to a street that spanned the southern length of another neighborhood. The number of scents he'd be processing from walking that street would increase his chances of finding the ones he was looking for, though from what he'd already experienced, they'd have to be within a few streets north of him.

With the time already approaching 1:00 p.m., Alex mapped out his planned route: follow the road until he could make a right turn, then turn back and check the three rows of houses south of the street in front of his old middle school. If he found nothing, head home and relax a bit, then come back without Bailey, possibly with his motorcycle.

After a shortcut through a nearby parking lot, Alex stuck to the south part of the street. With Bailey matching his walking pace, he closed his eyes and focused on the scents coming south. Like the streets he'd already walked, an assortment of scents from animal fur, construction tools, paints, car exhaust and fluids, fresh groceries, lawn products, asphalt, and various kinds of decay--among others--drew the attention of his olfactory sense. Though he continued to give the weakest ones the most attention, none blew past that matched Shane's scents, and before long, he had passed the intersection leading north.

Once at the southward street ahead, and after a final sniff, Alex crossed the street and headed back, turning north into the neighborhood at the street he passed. With it intersecting the next street at the halfway point, he looked left and right before deciding to go left and then double back at the corner. The numerous residents outside, doing everything from playing to working, acknowledged him when he came close, the one kid he saw playing with a giant rubber ball calling out to Bailey once he saw him.

"Yeah, he's a good boy," Alex said as he walked past.

At the end of the street, he walked forward enough to look down the length of the intersecting one. Several more residents were outside, and two cars were coming his way, one that pulled onto the next street north. With the winds now feeling a bit more southeast than west, Alex walked as far west as he could, but found no hint of Shane.

On his way back, a wave of fresh grocery scents wafted past him. At first the cold deli meat got his attention and made him lick his lips, but then came

Shane's human scent. Alex came to a stop and told Bailey to do the same. With another sniff, he confirmed it. Shane was either outside, or had opened a window.

"C'mon, boy." Hoping he wouldn't lose his chance, Alex increased his pace after crossing the street. When Bailey came close to running past him, Alex matched him, turning the corner onto the next street and keeping up their speed until the next street north. Once there, he slowed and got Bailey to do likewise, before pulling his phone out and staring down the street.

The houses that felt like the source of the scent both had a minivan parked in their driveways, but only one had both its rear door up and hints of grocery bags inside. After a few seconds of watching, Shane emerged from the other side of that same minivan, and Alex's pulse rose.

So that's where he lives. Pleased that that mystery was solved, Alex waited to see if Shane would notice him. Nothing about his behavior before he walked away with bags in his hands implied he did. "Bailey, let's go," Alex said with a tug on Bailey's leash. As he made his way closer to Shane's house, he kept note of the numbers on the curbs. *533... 529... 525. Got it.*

At the same time, and with every step, he could feel his heart racing in his ears and neck. He pushed his sunglasses up a bit and kept his phone in a position like he was watching it more than everything else. Soon, Alex was almost directly south of the house, and as he watched, Shane reemerged through the front entrance.

As Shane looked up, and then in his direction, his sudden stop, and the shifting of his expression from blank to surprised, made holding back the many kinds of expressions Alex felt ready to display difficult. At least until, after a few seconds, Shane glanced at the minivan, and then made a beeline for him.

Despite the setting and time of day, some level of concern filled Alex's head as he approached. "Are you happy now?" Shane asked once he was close enough for his lowered voice to still carry a frustrated, possibly confrontational, tone.

Alex forced himself to speak, to not let Shane dominate things. "Not a hundred percent."

Shane huffed out his nose and shook his head.

By then, Bailey's tail was no longer wagging, his attention fixed on Shane. "Especially not after what Dad just told me."

"Did he figure out I was there?"

"No. More canine units are being called in, and patrols are increasing."

Shane, after a second, glanced back at his house, and then stayed quiet.

"I don't know about you, but I don't see that as good. Especially not if bloodhounds get involved."

"You think they're going to follow you to where you live?"

"You think they can't? Or won't? And what about you?"

"Even if they did," Shane said before looking at himself, "do either of us look anything like what the cops are looking for?"

"Not yet, and what happens when every place around here with animals starts being watched, if they're not already?"

"Then don't go out until two or so in the morning, and don't panic so much."

Alex glanced towards Shane's house before he replied. "Somehow, I get the feeling this'll only be my problem." Shane had no chance to respond before the sound of a door opening drew the attention of both of them.

The woman that emerged from the house, Alex suspected, was about as old as his mother; her short hair, like Shane's, was jet black. After she noticed and focused on them, the scents the open door had released reached Alex's nose.

As he processed them, his flesh tightened from a sudden chill, and his heartrate rose. Shane's werewolf scent wasn't the only one the house contained.

When the woman spoke up in a friendly greeting, Alex offered a wave, but didn't smile. "Shane, what's left in there?"

"Just boxes," Shane called back before returning his focus to Alex. "You're making your own problems by worrying so much."

"Not what I'm talking about." Alex replied once the house's front door was closed and the scents from inside had blown away. "It's that meat you had." Shane didn't respond right away, and Alex capitalized on it. "You got that from someone, and I'm pretty certain you can rely on that and stay inside. I can't, and guess who made things harder by killing so many animals before?"

Shane remained quiet after Alex finished, though the change in Shane's expression, and eventual pace back across the street, said everything. He was pissed but letting it out in ways besides words. Unable to hear anything that he said to his mother, if anything, Alex turned his attention back to Bailey and rubbed his head and ears.

Once Shane and his mother were both inside, Alex told Bailey to follow him and then started the walk back home.

* * *

He turned onto his street just before his phone sounded the IM tone. A minute before, he'd messaged Nathan, Catherine, and Marcus all at once, saying that he'd found Shane's house.

Catherine W.: Are you serious? Where?

Alex S.: Yeah. Rozelle Avenue.

Catherine W.: Where's that?

Nathan T.: Near our old middle school. Like two streets away.

Alex S.: Yeah.

Catherine W.: What happened?

Alex quickly decided against mentioning the second werewolf scent.

Alex S.: He came up to me, we had some back and forth, and then I called him on something and he walked off.

Catherine W.: On what?

Alex S.: On killing so many animals. More police are coming in.

Nathan T.: Oh, boy.

Alex S.: Yeah. No thanks to him.

Until Alex reached the front door of his house, the texts stopped.

Marcus A.: How did you find him?

Alex S.: I could smell him a few streets off.

Marcus A.: Right place, right time?

Alex S.: More or less. First time it happened, I found his scent near our middle school. Figured he lived nearby.

Marcus A.: Makes sense.

Nathan T.: You said more police. Just police?

Alex S.: No. More canines too.

Nathan T.: Oh, man.

Catherine W.: But, isn't that just an issue when...you know.

Alex S.: I don't think so. I've seen some officers driving around with them, and this guy, and me, smell strange regardless.

Catherine W.: Then what happens if they track you?

Alex S.: No idea. Might ask Dad.

The texts went silent again after that, leaving Alex the rest of the day to consider what to say to his parents, and when.

It was before dinner was served that he decided to speak up, leading with the point that he'd found Shane's house. "No wonder you took such a long walk," his father said.

"But he found him."

"Yes, but strictly speaking, the *kid* hasn't done anything."

"And if he wound up in jail, the full moon would force him to change," Alex added.

"That too, so the only way I can see this going is he makes a mistake around one of my officers and gets killed. Unless he starts looking for animals elsewhere."

Alex felt a twinge of cold fear hit his chest at his father's statement. "I did what I could to warn him. He more or less blew me off."

"That's his problem, Son. Not yours."

"Did anything else come to mind today?" his mother asked.

"No. Couldn't think of anything else."

Sunday, October 16th, 2011
Moon Phase – Waning Gibbous

After awaking to Bailey lying by his side, Alex spent part of the morning skating up and down the street parallel to the back-alley Shane used to head home. Although he'd given the impression that he knew what he was doing, Alex struggled to figure out how, without following the route he used down the other street and along the creek, Shane had covered the distance between their houses without being seen.

Wonder if his mother picked him up as well as dropped him off. After reaching the south end of the street again, he glanced right. There were no streetlights between where he stood and the next intersection in that direction---more than enough distance for an SUV to quietly sit and await him. The time Shane had given him--6:15 p.m.--sprang back to mind as well, and after some time to process things, Alex found himself sighing.

The second werewolf then became a focus of his curiosity. Was it a sibling, extended relative, father, or someone else? As Alex returned home, his assumption leaned towards a sibling. How young or old they could be didn't feel too important to question, though he felt a shudder come on at the thought of it being a child.

* * *

It was nearing noon when the sound of the doorbell ringing jolted Bailey awake from his rest atop Alex's legs. Figuring it was the mailman, Alex let his mother answer it, but pulled one headphone cup off regardless.

"Can I help you? ... Yes. Why? ... About? ..." His father left his room before his mother spoke again, heading towards the front door. "Wait a minute. Wait a minute... Honey?" The nervous tone of his mother's voice pushed Alex to get up and follow his father.

And when he saw Shane standing at the door, his focus on anything but him was lost.

Chapter 16 – I'd Like You To...

Sunday, October 16th, 2011
Moon Phase – Waning Gibbous

"Why are you here?" was what Alex's father asked as he stood frozen in place.

"Not to cause trouble, sir. I swear," Shane said. His eye-contact towards Alex's father never wavered.

"Then spell it out for me: why are you here?"

Shane glanced towards Alex again. "Hey," he said before waving two fingers in front of his eyes. "Calm down a bit."

Alex closed his eyes and shook his head in response, just before his parents looked towards him. Once they reopened, his mother's expression shifted to concern and his tongue ran over his teeth.

As he tried to slow his breathing, despite his heart, Shane spoke again, his focus back on his father. "I just want to talk to him."

"Then you can do it with us nearby."

Shane stayed quiet for a moment, exhaling out his nose. "Alright. Right here, or inside?"

'Right here' was Alex's immediate choice, and when his father looked towards him again, he said so. Once he was standing between his parents and Shane, he asked, "What did you need?"

"You, for a few hours."

As Alex's eyebrows scrunched into a questioning scowl, his mother asked, "What for?"

"My parents want to meet him."

This time, Alex's father spoke. "For what reason?"

"All they said was, 'See if he's willing to come over for a while'."

Although Alex didn't notice any hints of maliciousness in Shane's tone, his father replied first, and how he expected. "No. Absolutely not."

Expecting Shane to protest, Alex kept quiet. Instead, Shane shrugged and said, "Alright." He then about-faced and walked away.

"C'mon, Son." Alex stepped back over the threshold and his father closed and locked the door. After a confused-sounding sigh, he asked, "Do you think that was what he wanted?"

"It sounded sincere, so probably."

"But why would he ask that now?" his mother asked.

"Because I found his house yesterday, and that made his folks nervous?"

"They could be thinking he'll identify them, or him, if another animal turns up dead," his father said after a second.

"Could be, but I don't know," Alex said.

"Didn't you say that would be dangerous?" his mother asked. "Him being arrested."

"Yeah, so it has to be some other reason."

"Whatever it is, Son, you know what he's done," his father said.

"And you don't know these people either," his mother added.

"That too, so don't get involved with them."

After Alex glanced outside, finding Shane already gone, he spoke. "If I see him again, I'll just tell him I won't say anything. Hopefully that'll work."

"If it doesn't, or he tells you there's another reason, you tell us."

Alex nodded his head and said he would, though for an hour after, he couldn't stop wondering why Shane had given up so easily. Was it concern for his family, or something else?

Monday, October 17th, 2011
Moon Phase – Waning Gibbous

"What do you think they wanted then?" Nathan asked once their class was over.

"Try to convince me to not rat them out, tell me that their son's not a bad guy? I don't know."

Nathan began to grin after a moment. "You say that, and now I'm imagining us in some TV police drama."

Alex gave a half smile at that. "Starting to wish this was nothing more than that."

"But anyway," Nathan said after he stopped grinning, "got any ideas for next time?"

"A few. None that won't make me a burden on my folks, though."

"What about scouting a spot and then going for it?"

"Shane suggested the same thing, and going out very early in the morning, but it's the patrols I'm worried about. If I pick a spot, but then they're there that night, or use the canine units and track me, I'm screwed." As his friend went quiet, likely to think of other options, Alex added to his answer. "Plus, as Dad told me, the police are now actively looking for large canines."

"Shoot to kill?"

Alex shuddered at that. "I hope not, but for all I know, yes."

Nathan gave a nervous hum in response. "I'd say go out of town if it comes down to it. Did your folks say when they needed you to decide on something?"

Alex shook his head. "Kind of wish they did. I'm guessing around a week before the full moon is as long as they'll wait."

"When's that?"

"November tenth. It's a Thursday."

Nathan took a second to respond. "If you can't decide on what to do by then, tell me. There's a few places with livestock around here."

The offer eased some of Alex's mental weight. "Thanks, man. I appreciate it."

Nathan nodded in response, though as he and Alex approached the nearest stairwell, he resumed speaking. "Just thought of something. This guy lives in a house in town. How long has he been living there?"

"Good question," Alex said after a second. The fact that he'd not thought about that before now, even though he couldn't see Shane letting slip how long he'd lived there, made him feel foolish. But if he and his family had been there for some time... What if they'd always been there, but just more careful until just before Angela died?

What her connection was to Shane and his family stayed on Alex's thoughts as Nathan spoke again. "Has to be a while, a few months at least."

"Or more."

"Yeah, but if that's so, he did a really good job hiding the evidence up until now."

Or he never killed anything himself until that calf. "Or went after things other than livestock." Alex noticed Nathan rub his arms after that statement.

"That the impression you've got of him?"

"Him being a man-eater? No. I meant stray animals, things like that."

"Ugh."

"Would be easy to hide."

"Yeah, it would, but that sounds like something to do if you're low on options and need something fast."

"Yeah," Alex said after a second. "If I can get him to spill anything, I'll let you know." After Nathan gave him a quick handshake, the two of them parted ways.

* * *

As the first half-hour of his shift went by, despite the help he was providing to the shoppers, Alex found himself more lost in thinking about everything from the last few days. Although he was quite certain of what Shane's parents wanted of him, he couldn't let himself think that was the whole of it. Nathan's offer remained hopeful for the time it stayed in mind, though it soon gave way to something else: the meat that Shane had given him.

If that was how Shane, Angela, and the third werewolf had stayed out of sight and kept from killing, what had caused them to go after the calf? Lapse in supply? Boredom? He was asked by Daniel to help at the front as he tried to think of a third possibility. None came to mind, even ten minutes later, though those same ten minutes gave him enough time to lean towards boredom.

As 5:00 p.m. and the last hour of his shift neared, Alex turned his attention to the trade shelves. What few gaps he found were closed, though as he worked, he almost missed seeing someone with jet-black hair walking by the store. The door's bell went off soon after, and when Daniel greeted the customer, the replying voice was enough to tell Alex that it was Shane.

Alex felt his chest at that and attempted to resume working, only to stop himself after a few seconds. If Shane was already here, then he had a chance to assure him he wasn't going to rat him out, possibly find out more about what his parents wanted.

After a few steps towards the front windows, Alex noticed Shane heading towards the used RPG rulebook shelves, his attention solely on them. With Daniel manning the register and counter, he kept his distance, but left an eye on Shane.

Although he didn't move, Alex was quick to doubt that he'd come here on his own. With a glance outside through the nearest window, in the direction he'd seen Shane approach from, he couldn't see anything like the

SUV his mother had driven; the occupied parking spaces near the store obstructed his view of the rest of the lot and encouraged him to move.

The glance he snuck at Shane as he walked past was returned. Was he waiting for some of the customers to leave, or for him to be in a more secluded spot?

After seeing nothing from the north side of the store, Alex was asked for some input from a nearby customer. By the time he'd finished helping them, Shane had come closer, and then within a few feet. "Question for you," he began as Alex's previous customer walked away, "I'm looking for a certain trade. Could you help me?"

"Yeah," Alex said after glancing at Daniel. Shane had started moving before he finished the word, and led him to the other side of the store, where at least one shelf hid him from Daniel's view. "I'm not---" Alex began, to which Shane cut him off.

"Yes, they're serious about meeting you. No, it's not a trap or some kind of bait, but yes, they will mind if you say no."

The last part of Shane's statement elevated Alex's pulse. Was he bluffing? What would his parents do if he wasn't? With his suspicions about their intent now sealed, what he told his parents was next out of his mouth. "I'm not about to identify you, or get you tossed in jail."

"That's not what they're concerned about."

"Then why didn't you say that before instead of being so vague?"

"Because I figured you already knew how stupid an idea that would be."

Alex glanced around before continuing. "If it's that important, then at least give me some idea of what they want."

"Like I said, they just want to talk to you. That's it. About what, I don't know. They didn't tell me."

Alex let his shoulders slump. "So, this has nothing to do with me finding your place the other day? They just suddenly want to."

"The fact that you did made them a bit nervous, yes. And me too."

"So you were concerned that I would say something."

"Were. Not 'still am'," Shane replied.

"Then I guess what I said about the patrols and canine units are factors too."

"Yes." Shane's reply came with a reluctant sigh.

If that's what's concerning his parents, but he knows I won't speak up... "You called me a rogue before. Is that what this is about? You all trying to convince me to go along with you?"

"No."

"Then why is it such a big deal that I talk to your folks? I know what I shouldn't be doing. What is there to discuss?"

"You know what you shouldn't be doing, and yet you lost your catch and almost let yourself go hungry. And then you make a fuss about being left in the dark, even though you already knew what could happen in that case." Shane paused, and then continued before Alex could rebut, though as he spoke, his frustrated tone grew a touch of disgust. "Here. As simple as I can make it. My old man gave up some of our meat stock for you, made me carry it to your house and offer it because they were worried you would kill someone. That's why they'll mind if you say no."

After Shane spoke, the reference to his father and what had been done pushed Alex into thinking he was the second werewolf. At the same time, the fact that he'd not brought up the meat the day before put his sudden departure when turned down into context. If he'd pushed or brought that up...but now this was sounding like a demand, and that wouldn't have sat well with his folks nearby.

"You're making this sound like an obligation."

"It's not, but are you honestly saying you can't spare an hour or so after that?" Alex delayed too long. "Wednesday. Between one and four p.m. Could you make that?"

Although what he'd promised his folks had returned to mind by that point, the time and date Shane had given him would be when both of them would be at work, and when neither work nor his classes would be things to consider. "Let me think on it."

Chapter 17 – ...Meet The Family

Monday, October 17th, 2011
Moon Phase – Waning Gibbous

When Shane said nothing in response, and showed no hint of being insulted at the statement, Alex went back to work. Two days. No obligation maybe, but now he couldn't shake the feeling of something happening if he refused. And then, how long would Shane's parents want him over, and what kinds of things would they bring up with him?

As though he could sense his discomfort, Shane approached him again several minutes later. "Just show up if you decide you want to," he said once Alex's focus was on him.

"And if I don't?"

"Then I guess you're not only a rogue, but an ungrateful one." Though Shane walked away before Alex could retort, after he was outside, Alex tailed him until he could see the SUV his mother was driving. She drove off shortly after looking at the store's front, though her expression made Alex feel like she was looking directly at him.

For the remainder of the day, outside of dinner with his folks, he kept to himself. Asking his friends for their inputs crossed his mind several times, but once his phone was in his hand and the instant messenger opened, he reconsidered it.

At the same time, Alex had been considering telling his parents what really happened that day. Even if it wasn't something Shane or his family were planning to exploit, there was no sense holding up the fib now.

As he worked up the courage to tell his parents, Alex heard the TV in the living room switch on. A laugh-track sounded shortly after, along with his mother giggling. Hoping some humor might diminish any strong emotions they would have, he let the program run a few minutes before getting up, and then diverting into the bathroom. A few sighs later, he walked into the living room and waited for his folks to acknowledge him.

"Could you mute that? I need to tell you both something," Alex said.

"Did you come up with something?" his mother asked once the TV was muted.

"No, it's something else." Alex got no response and continued. "That dog I said I killed? Never happened." The lack of horror in favor of confusion on the faces of his parents was a slight relief.

"You went that whole day hungry?" his father asked, to which Alex shook his head.

"So then, what did you do?" his mother asked.

Alex closed his eyes and breathed out his nose before responding, reopening them halfway through. "That Shane kid. He fed me." When his parent's expressions shifted into shock, what he wanted to add never left his mouth.

"With what?" his father demanded.

"It…smelled like bovine meat."

"Are you sure?"

"Pretty. It was a big piece."

His father continued after a moment. "So, he was here before?"

"Yeah."

"In the house?"

A biting cold gripped Alex's chest. "No. I told him stay outside."

His father sighed. "When did he do this?"

"About two that day."

"In the afternoon?" his mother asked. Alex nodded. "That's crazy."

"I don't think he did it alone. Think his mother drove him here."

For a moment, everyone went silent. "Was that why you told me to stay inside?"

"Yeah. I just didn't want you seeing him and getting worried."

"Is that why he came here yesterday?"

Alex sighed after his father asked that, and looked away.

"It is, wasn't it?"

"Yeah."

"Why didn't you tell us?" his mother asked.

"Because he didn't make it clear until today."

"So then, is he still asking you to meet his parents?"

Alex nodded. "Because of that, and a few other things. They know I won't give him away."

"Then, I don't understand. There's nothing you need to say to them."

Alex shrugged. "Maybe he just wants me to thank his folks in person. Let them get to know me."

"Son, you're saying all this on speculation and spare details. Why is he not telling you exactly what he, or they, want? Why has he asked you about this twice in two days?"

"It's not all speculation, Dad. He's called me a rogue before, and now implied that I'm 'ungrateful' if I refuse to speak to his parents."

"Ungrateful?"

"I know. They made the choice to send him with the meat, though."

"So, for all you know, it's just him who has the problem with you doing that, not his parents."

Alex didn't answer, though he somewhat agreed with the assumption.

"Regardless, here's my suggestion: write them a 'Thank You' note and leave it in their mailbox. Done. He'll have no more reason to bother you after that."

"That did cross my mind."

His father nodded. "Just do that, Son. It's the best solution, I think."

"I think so too," his mother said.

Alex sighed. He wanted to agree more than that, but something in his gut told him that simply wouldn't cut it. Shane wouldn't have dropped a date and a time otherwise.

Wednesday, October 19th, 2011
Moon Phase – Last Quarter

Tuesday passed with him juggling what to do and weighing what his parents said versus Shane. By that same evening, he'd come close to deciding on what to do. Once his Wednesday class with Nathan was over, he nodded to him and parted ways, heading straight home to Bailey and a few minutes' walk with him.

The urge to say 'screw it' and just not go refused to fully leave his head, even after he'd sat in the kitchen stroking Bailey's head for several minutes. As 1:00 p.m. arrived, Alex couldn't bring himself to approach the front door. Shane had given him a timeframe, not a set time. The minutes continued to pass as he weighed his options again, all the while tension was building in his gut.

He saw no reason why he'd have to stay there past 4:00 p.m., but the second werewolf scent... If it was from Shane's father...and what would he be like? Had the "rogue" label come from him, or just Shane's anger?

After a lengthy sigh, Alex buried his face in his hands. Now he couldn't help thinking that if he went along with this meeting, he'd be at a major disadvantage, even in basic discussions.

As 1:30 p.m. drew closer, he pulled his phone out and wrote up a text telling Nathan to reply ASAP.

He did so several minutes later.

Nathan T.: Hey, man. What's going on?

Alex exhaled before typing out his response.

Alex S.: You working?

Nathan T.: Yeah, but it's not busy. Why?

Alex S.: I'm nervous about meeting Shane's parents.

Nathan's reply was swift.

Nathan T.: Are you serious!?

Alex S.: Yes.

When his friend didn't respond, he continued.

Alex S.: All I need is a small favor: Text me at 2:15, 3:00, and 3:45. Just a quick message to respond to.

Nathan T.: Just don't go, man. If you're that nervous, just stay home.

Alex S.: I was about to, but I'd rather get this guy off my back.

Nathan's response came after a minute.

Nathan T.: Alright. I'll do that.

Alex S.: Thanks, man.

Once he pocketed his phone, Alex gave Bailey one last headrub before leaving the house, his backpack and two cold water bottles in tow.

He arrived at Shane's house just before 1:45 p.m. Two vehicles sat in the driveway---the SUV he'd seen before, now blocked by a Jeep. Before opening his helmet's visor, he attempted to spot any movement by the windows. He could picture Shane just sitting by one of them, watching for him or the sound of his motorcycle, but nothing over the next minute confirmed it.

After a swig of water, he parked his motorcycle in the street, and then made his way to the front door. He could feel his skin chilling with every step, and didn't take his helmet off until he'd depressed the doorbell and then stepped back.

It was Shane who answered the door, and Alex huffed out his nose when his mother asked who it was. "Alex," Shane said, and then gestured him inside. Already, Alex had noticed both Shane's and the second werewolf's scents, both of which made him quiver as he crossed the door's threshold. "Calm down, will you?" Shane said as he closed the door behind him.

The response Alex wanted to give came only from a quick huff out his nose.

"Fine. Just wait here then." As Shane left, Alex tried to glance around and take in the place. Despite the several musty scents among the many others, the place looked nice and well-kept. The emergency responder duffle bag in the foyer drew his attention next; the Sugar Land city logo and crimson red color screamed "EMT".

When Shane returned, Alex's attention was ripped away from the bag. "C'mon, in here," Shane said with another gesture to follow. Alex obliged after a second glance at the front door.

He rounded the corner to find both of Shane's parents sitting at what looked like a dining table, already staring in the direction he was coming from. It took only a second more for his memory to be jogged, and for a hand to unconsciously move near his mouth.

Shane's father was the EMT. One of the four who had helped Angela the night he and Nathan had found her.

As both of Shane's parents greeted him, his gaze moved to Shane and then back to his father. His throat stayed locked as he recalled what his father had told him about Angela's body going missing, his eyes squeezing shut as his sense of unease built by the second.

"What's wrong with him?" he heard Shane's mother ask.

"Probably worked himself---" Shane began.

"Shane, wait," his father said. Alex wanted nothing else than to back away when the silence came; he was one step into it before Shane's father continued. "Alex, calm down."

Fat fucking chance, Alex thought as his eyes reopened. He then focused on Shane, his tongue resting near his potential fangs. *No wonder you were so evasive.*

"Alex, listen to me," Shane's father said. "If you freak out and change, you're on your own."

"Meaning you're walking home in broad daylight, hungry." Shane added with a stern edge to his tone. "Or is that---"

"Shane, don't," his mother said before getting up from her chair. As she approached, she continued. "Just calm down, Alex. Please."

Alex swallowed in response. No blood on his tongue, or fangs, yet. The tension around his chest was still great, though.

More seconds went by, though the family stayed silent. When Shane attempted to get a look at Alex's eyes, he shut them and shook his head, prompting Shane's mother to continue. "A talk with you is all we want."

"Which I told him," Shane said.

"Hang on, you two," Shane's father said after a second. "I think I know why he's freaking out."

I wouldn't doubt it.

"Alex, if it'll help you relax, yes, I took Angela's body from the hospital that night, but only because I couldn't allow her body to be used for organ donations. There'd be more werewolves because of her."

Alex huffed out his nose again, though his chest tension laxed some at hearing that.

"I felt sorry for her too, but I couldn't risk that."

"He won't believe you, Dad." Shane said.

"Maybe, maybe not, but that's the truth." He then went silent again.

Alex closed his eyes again, breathing out his nose once more. The admission was a relief to hear, and he heard nothing in the father's voice to make him think he was being deceitful. But in the back of his mind, he felt sick at the idea of keeping that knowledge to himself, good reason or not.

"We didn't bury her, or burn her, or dump her or some crap like that," Shane said, to which his mother said his name. "Bottom line: we didn't disrespect her."

Wishing he had a way of knowing if that was true, Alex felt his heartrate slow a few beats. When a hand was placed on his shoulder shortly after, Shane's mother spoke. "Are you okay?"

Alex exhaled again, not willing to speak just yet and opting for a shake of his head.

"Then, if you need some time, go home and then come back. We'll wait."

Chapter 18 – The Cards On The Table

Wednesday, October 19th, 2011
Moon Phase – Last Quarter

Before Alex got far into thinking about the positives of that action, he heard his phone sound the IM tone, and his eyes snapped to it. Despite knowing that if he stalled too long Nathan would start to worry, his nerves kept him from pulling it out of his pocket.

"Answer it if you need to," Shane's mother said. Alex still didn't move until he spotted Shane's hand moving towards his phone. The growl he wanted to sound kept within his lungs, though Shane retracted his hand as soon as the phone was out of his pocket.

The message Nathan had sent was a bit more involved than he expected, but after a second to think, that made him feel safer overall.

Nathan T.: Question: What was that mod
you found for DOOM? That ultra-violent one?

Alex S.: Brutal DOOM

Nathan T.: Thanks

"So I'm not the only one around here who likes that." Shane's statement drew Alex's gaze for a moment.

"Likes what?" his father asked.

"Something Alex's friend mentioned."

As Alex sighed to himself, Shane's mother repeated what she'd said about choosing to leave for a while. Several hours was what he felt he needed, and by that point a later date to meet would be necessary.

"Or I could just stand outside with him for a few minutes," Shane suggested. Alex glanced at him, the silence from Shane's parents an obvious tell. With sweat beading under his hair, he soon broke his board-stiff stance to wipe it away, before taking no more than a seconds' glance at Shane's parents. Though neither of them seemed ready to pressure him on the idea, he started moving a few seconds later, the red around his ears losing its intensity at the same time.

Shane stuck close at first, so close that Alex was left wondering if he was trying to listen to his heartbeat, before rushing ahead and grabbing the door handle. Outside, Shane stood downwind of him, not speaking in favor of leaning against one of the porch's support posts. Not being able to see the faces of his parents or pick up their scents allowed much of the tension around Alex's chest to dissolve as the seconds passed. Enough that even though his motorcycle was less than ten yards away, he made no effort to approach it.

"Calmed down yet?" Shane asked after a minute.

Alex only glanced at him.

"That's a 'no', then."

Piss off, Alex thought before wondering if he'd been reeking of fear up to just then.

"The sooner you go back in there, the sooner it'll be over."

"Like I don't know that," Alex at last replied, a slight growl accompanying his words.

"So, what's stopping you? Is it my folks or something else? The scents in the house?"

When Shane said that, Alex slipped his backpack off in favor of speaking. His water bottles were tucked away in the same pocket that the tennis ball was, and with a squeeze of the open backpack, Bailey's scents reached his nostrils. Although they helped, now he couldn't help imagining having him nearby, and how much nicer that would've been.

"Thought so." Shane said as Alex took several drinks from the bottles.

"It's not one thing, alright?"

"It's her too, isn't it?" Shane didn't wait for an answer. "Remember when I said I bit you to make sure you knew what was coming?" He paused. "You still think I was bullshitting you?"

"What I think is you could've been wrong."

"Then, when you go back in there, ask."

Alex didn't respond right away. As long as it had been since the night he'd been bitten, he couldn't see Shane and his father not having talked about what happened, or having decided on what to say if questioned about it. "Just like that?"

"If it's still bothering you."

"Maybe." Another minute passed with neither him nor Shane speaking. Thirty-five minutes remained until Nathan's next check-in, making the idea of waiting until then feel more like a giveaway than a good idea. Shane's parents hadn't stopped him the last time he answered the text, but then, Shane had watched him type the response... *Like he'll figure it out.*

Alex spent another few minutes outside before turning toward the door. Shane led him back inside, into the same scents that had made him nervous before, and continued to stand nearby as Alex adjusted. He soon tapped Alex's backpack, causing him to unzip a pocket and puff some of Bailey's scent from it. It helped, though nowhere near as much as before.

"Ready?" Shane asked.

Despite the increased pace of his heart and shaky breathing, after a few seconds, Alex responded. "I guess."

"Good enough. C'mon." Alex exhaled once before following Shane towards the living room. Though the sight of his father froze him in place again, Shane was quick to notice and suggest something. "Maybe we should go somewhere else and talk to him?"

"He's fine, Shane," his father replied.

"Not if he's that easily scared."

"Shane. Be patient." After a few seconds, he stood up from the table he was sitting at. "I'm just moving to the couch," he said to Alex, whose attention never left him as he did so and slipped into the spot he wanted. "That second couch? When you're ready, just sit down."

"Shane," his mother began, "let's get some waters ready."

As Shane and his mother left the room, the tension Alex thought would vanish grew in strength. Now it was just him and Shane's old man. Nothing about his expression or posture was overtly dangerous or threatening, but Alex's throat remained locked up, as though a single wrong word would cause him trouble. With what he'd said to Shane about being patient, the idea of leaving and coming back had suddenly become more appealing.

"On second thought," Shane's father said after a moment, "excuse me. Be right back." Again, Alex watched him get up and then make his way towards the left side of the house. Other than the sounds of water running and ice clinking in the next room, he was now alone. And in turn, he couldn't help feeling like this was something Shane's father was counting on: him relaxing first before they all came back into the room, possibly one by one.

Alex snuck another look at his phone. 2:41 p.m. Still a while before Nathan would text him again. The couch he'd been directed towards was a two-seater, facing away from the direction Shane's father would approach from when he returned. Whatever had pulled him out of the room, Alex was certain he couldn't stall that long.

Then the sounds from clinking ice and running water stopped, and it was Shane who walked the four glasses into the room and set them down on the table in front of both couches. The seat he then took was as close to the other as he could get. *Guess he's not gonna move from there.*

Alex then noticed Shane's mother watching him from the kitchen. Despite how quiet she was, how concerned she appeared dug the same feelings of guilt into Alex's head that he'd felt the night his folks found out he was a werewolf. Unlike then, however, the feelings were quicker to fade. As they did, enough of his fears were siphoned away that he took a step toward the two-seater, reconsidering for only a moment before continuing.

It was as he sat down that his concern, and his heartrate, spiked again. The loud, leathery squeaking of the cushion came across like a signal that he'd made himself vulnerable.

"Keep it together," Shane said, drawing Alex's gaze. As a door opened elsewhere in the house, Shane kept talking. "Or do you need a few more minutes?"

Alex sighed and said nothing as the footsteps from Shane's father came closer. He kept him in the corner of his eye as he passed, but instead of sitting on the couch again, he joined his wife in the kitchen.

After the two of them exchanged a hug, he faced Alex and waited for his gaze to be met. "Like she told you, we just wanted you here for a talk. Nothing one-sided and we're not going to demand you do anything, but I'm sure you understand why I can't let myself or my son be put behind bars."

Alex nodded. Despite the even tone, his throat gained a knot in response.

"I'm assuming your parents already know, but have you told anyone else?" Alex almost shook his head. As Shane began to speak for him, his father shushed him. "Let him do it."

After a few more seconds, and a swallow, Alex nodded.

"And you trust them, a hundred percent?"

That question briefly sparked doubt in Alex's head, but he nodded again.

"I'm assuming you thought it over for awhile? Or did something happen that made you say something?"

Shane's glance at his father directed Alex's thoughts to his defensive shift incident. Was he asking that to get him to speak in detail, or did Shane keep the incident to himself? Though leaning towards the latter, and unable to see only a nod working here, Alex did it anyway.

"Which was it?"

Within a second, Alex felt the attention on him burrow under his skin. The only word he said after several more seconds was, "Both."

At that, Shane nodded. Likely his way of confirming, or implying 'That's a start'.

"I see," Shane's father replied. "Unless you want to, you don't need to tell us the details."

Wasn't planning on it.

After a second, Shane's mother chimed in. "From what Shane has told us, you're doing alright. Is that true?"

Alex immediately frowned and locked his gaze on Shane. "What?" he asked after a second, to which Alex huffed and shook his head. "You seemed like it to me. What, would you rather I said you weren't?"

"Shane," his father began, "he's likely still frustrated that this happened to him."

That's a fucking understatement. Alex felt his throat unclench some, and before Shane retorted, he spoke. "Didn't need to."

"What?" Shane's father asked.

"He said 'didn't need to'," Shane clarified. "He thinks if I hadn't bitten him, he'd be fine."

Instead of immediately replying, Shane's father shifted his attention between Alex and Shane, his wife laying a hand on his before he exhaled at length. Meanwhile, Alex was bracing for what Shane's father would say. As confident as Shane had sounded before, his gut still told him he was right.

That was when an IM chime from his phone sounded, and his attention broke. This time, he didn't delay on reaching for it and ignoring Shane as best he could.

Nathan T.: I think Marcus might like
this more than me.

Alex S.: Probably. He does enjoy

Duke Nukem a lot.

Nathan T.: Yeah.

Expecting to be asked who he'd texted, Alex refocused on Shane after his phone was put up, but was asked nothing.

"If that's what you think, Alex, then I'll tell you this: I can't agree with either you or my son a hundred percent. I wasn't there. I didn't see anything that happened."

Alex closed his eyes and hung his head in response.

"Dad, I told you---"

"I know, Shane, but you didn't tell us until after you did it."

That figures, Alex thought as he buried his face behind his hands. The familiar scents stuck to his skin provided a bit of calm.

"And I explained myself. To him too."

"How well, though?"

Alex's attention was taken at that. 'How well?' What else was there to mention?

When Shane didn't respond quick enough, his mother took over. "What did Shane tell you?"

After a sigh and repositioning of his hands, Alex responded. "That he bit me because she bled on me."

"Nothing else?" After Alex shook his head, his fear growing about what he might hear, Shane's father took over. "Then it's probably best you hear the rest from me." He paused. "As Shane told us, your scent surfaced after he'd bitten you. That's why he was certain he wasn't doing anything to you beyond warning you."

Right away, Alex noticed the flaw in the logic. Once he could speak, he went after it. "That's still after."

"I know, and that's why I can't fully agree with you or my son. Either of you could be right. That said, your...shepherd, I believe? He started getting suspicious of you after a few days, didn't he?"

As Alex thought back, he couldn't recall Bailey being anything close to suspicious within the days following him being bitten, or even being in contact with Angela's blood. "No," he said with a shake of his head. He got no response and continued. "Not until I was a week from changing."

"If you'd waited that long for a clue---" Shane began before his parents shushed him.

"Unexplained anxiety, a more sensitive nose, and nightvision aren't clues?"

"By themselves, no," Shane retorted.

"That's stupid. Of course they'd be."

"Then how would you have explained all of that if I'd never bitten you?" Shane gave Alex three seconds, continuing when he didn't reply. "You'd be convinced you were going crazy or your body was mutating."

"So, it never occurred to you to wait just a bit longer and be a hundred percent sure? Maybe my 'scent' proved it because you scared the shit out of me."

Shane's eyes rolled. "Please, not that 'You could've spoken to me' horseshit again."

"Shane. Alex. Both of you knock it off," Shane's father demanded. He waited longer than Alex was comfortable with before speaking again, though Alex swore he noticed Shane flinch when the demand was made and pulled some satisfaction from it. "Good. That's enough of that." He paused again. "Now, Alex, there's another reason why we wanted you here."

Alex's pulse shot up, despite what he'd been told.

"My wife and I have been thinking about what you told our son before. About the canine units and increase in police patrols. I didn't expect canine units to be an issue, but since they now are, you've got to stay off the streets."

Easier said than done. Alex echoed that statement when he next spoke, adding, "That hunger will still be an issue."

"I know, and that's why we think you should come here when it surfaces."

At first Alex's eyes widened, but then he recalled the slab he'd been given. Shane spoke up as he remained silent. "And let him become dependent on us?"

"Shane, for the moment, and the foreseeable future, it's the safest idea." Shane's father paused again. "What I'm saying, Alex, is if you want to get the meat you need from us, I'll be happy to provide. It won't be free, though. You'll have to pay us for it and come here for it, but you'll always have enough."

The measure of weight that lifted from Alex's chest at that offer made the suggested cost of $75 per month sound like a pittance, and a slight smile worked its way onto his face.

Chapter 19 - A Deal Set

Wednesday, October 19th, 2011
Moon Phase – Last Quarter

When Alex was asked if the terms of the deal were fair, how relieved he was made answering far easier. "Yeah, that's perfect."

"Good to know," Shane's father said. "Just have the money ready at least a week before the full moon."

"And if you don't wake up early enough, have a ride ready," Shane said.

"How early? Two a.m.?"

"On the tenth of next month," Shane continued as Alex reached for his phone. "Just trust me. That's the date."

"Alright, I'll be ready." The room went silent after that, but a glance at Shane showed no hint of a reason. When Alex's thoughts fell back on his parents, the idea of telling them about the arrangement felt less nerve-wracking than he expected. His friends, however...

"Something bothering you?" Shane's mother asked.

Alex glanced at her, then shook his head. "Not really." When Shane's expression twitched, as though he was watching for something he could comment on, Alex continued. "Thank you for the offer."

"Is it your parents, or your friends?" Shane asked after his parents accepted the thanks. He continued when Alex didn't answer fast enough. "If you have to, just tell them it's your choice. Otherwise, don't say anything."

"Even though one of them figured out what happened before I said anything?"

Shane shrugged. "Like I said, but do what you want."

As Alex's gaze drifted to Shane's parents, his father spoke. "Was that all they figured out?"

Alex shook his head in response.

"Then am I correct to assume everyone you know knows about the hunger?"

"Yeah."

Shane's father hummed at first. "If Shane's idea sounds too blunt, you could tell them you found a supplier, and simply leave out any further details."

Alex mulled over the suggestion for a bit. A supplier sounded reasonable, though he couldn't see Nathan leaving it at that. If he spoke up, anyway. "I'll think about it," he said, to which Shane's father nodded.

"In the meantime, did you have anything you wanted to ask us?"

Alex lifted his head again. As Shane's parents came back into his view, a few things did come to mind.

How long had they lived here?

What had prompted Shane to go after Angela, or suddenly start killing animals when they had the meat to live off of?

Was there something he still didn't know about his lycanthropy?

With Shane so close, Alex tucked away anything he thought of concerning him. Before he could settle on a subject, Shane's mother continued. "You can ask us later if you're still nervous."

As the thought of willingly returning to the house for reasons beyond paying Shane's father entered his head, Alex stayed quiet and still until Nathan's third text came. After a few seconds, he checked it.

Nathan T.: Question: You still have that Vampire rulebook?

Alex S.: Mage, you mean.

Nathan T.: Oh, right. Never mind.

"I'll bet he wants to know about us more than anything," Shane said as Alex set his phone aside, drawing his attention.

"If so…" Shane's father began before stopping himself. "Well, let's leave that up to him."

Shane shrugged. "Alright."

For a moment after Shane spoke, Alex wanted to say he was ready to leave. After a lengthy, muffled sigh, and with one hand massaging his forehead, he pushed the tension from being center of attention aside as best he could. "I aware of it all?" he soon asked after slurring one word.

"What?" Shane asked.

"Being a werewolf. What don't I know?"

Shane glanced back at his father, the two of them matching gazes for a second. "I'm not sure." His father said. "You've changed at least twice... Does something not make sense?"

Alex threw out the first answer he could think of. "Timeframe."

"Timeframe? You mean when you'll change?" He continued after Alex nodded. "Oh, that's simple to remember. It's every twenty-nine days, minus about six to seven hours. You changed around three-thirty p.m. the first time, right?" Alex nodded again. "And then it happened about eight-forty a.m. the next time. See how it goes?"

"Expect it around one-fifty a.m. next time," Shane said. Alex made a mental note.

"The timeframe threw me off at first too, but it'll feel like a routine at some point. Even the thirty-six hours that you stay changed."

When things went quiet again, Alex noticed Shane squint a bit. "If you're still fretting about the 'animal hunger', don't. Just eat when you feel it. Done. No stress."

The shit did that come from? Alex tucked his potential remark aside, though something else about Shane's response began to stand out within a second: "when you feel it".

"I can't pre-empt that?"

Shane's father shook his head in response. "I've tried."

Alex returned his attention to Shane. "Then, what were you doing following me that night?"

"You had the same idea as me, just like I said."

"Somehow, I don't believe that."

"Then you don't have to."

Alex snuck a glance at Shane's father after that. He didn't seem agitated, though Alex felt the urge to leave returning. "May I?" he asked after a bit of silence, and after a glance to his right.

"Yes, if you're ready," Shane's father said.

"Thank you for coming by and speaking with us," his mother added as Shane stood up and headed for the entryway. Alex only stood up after returning the thanks and saying he'd have the money soon, a measure of warmth seeping into his skin when he felt out of their sight.

Shane waited until they were outside and the door was closed to speak. "Remember what I said: just keep it to yourself."

"We'll see how long that lasts," Alex said before slipping his helmet back on.

"So long as you don't give them reason to worry about you, it won't be an issue."

"Doing my best not to." Deciding not to remark further, Alex gave Shane a glance before walking off toward his motorcycle. As soon as he was home, he called Bailey over to enjoy his company, though the foreign scents on his clothing held his pet's attention for awhile.

Although bringing the visit up with his folks that night was simple to avoid, Nathan resumed texting him just before they came home.

Nathan T.: So, what happened?

> Alex S.: It was like he said: his
> folks just wanted to talk.

Nathan T.: Learn anything from them?

> *Alex S.*: A couple things. Won't have
> to guess when I'll shift anymore.

Nathan T.: Good to hear.

> *Alex S.*: Nice work with those texts
> before, man. Thanks.

Nathan T.: You're welcome.

The texts stopped for a minute.

Nathan T.: Question: had any more ideas about…you know.

For a moment, Alex felt his resolve about keeping the deal hidden weaken.

> *Alex S.*: Looking into a few. I'll let
> you know.

He got no response, and figured his friend was satisfied.

Friday, October 21th, 2011
Moon Phase – Waning Crescent

As Thursday passed with no questioning from either his parents or his friends, even with Marcus working with him throughout his shift that day, Alex grew more hopeful that, at best, he'd have to use the 'supplier' line, at least with his friends; his parents would see right through it.

Friday he was again left unquestioned by Nathan, both before and after class. His mindset then was more on when the next Mage session could take place, to which Alex expressed hope that next week would work.

That evening, as his father was getting ready for his shift, Alex heard him enter his room. After turning to face him, he was asked what he had figured his folks were curious about. "Have you heard anything from Shane?"

Alex shook his head.

"You think he'll still try and approach you?"

"Maybe, but if he does, he'll have nothing to stand behind."

His father kept quiet for a second. "What about this coming full moon? Any ideas yet?"

Although leaning towards saying 'No', Alex couldn't help thinking back on the 'supplier' fib Shane's father had brought up. And then something clicked.

"One." Alex got no answer and continued. "Maybe a meat supplier?"

His father hummed. "That makes sense..." His tone was just what Alex wanted, relaxing his tightened gut. "I'll see what my officers can tell me about such a thing."

"I'll see if I can find a company that'll do that, for a good price anyway."

"Let your mother and I know if and when you do." Alex then nodded and stood up to give his father a hug.

Saturday, October 22nd, 2011
Moon Phase – Waning Crescent

With a seven-hour shift at Blue Moon the next day, Alex kept sneaking listens to the session Trevor had going on in the back room. The four players were investigating the source of an undead scourge, something that got Marcus to remark with, "It always comes from the graveyard."

"Or some witch's hut, or a secret necromancer," Alex replied. "You going to join once you're off?"

"Maybe. Fourth edition's not my bag."

"Mine either, but..."

"Give it a few weeks. Trevor'll change the system." After Alex replied that he hoped it was to World of Darkness, Marcus changed the subject. "On that, since I'm leaving in an hour, you want your break now?"

"Sure, why not?" Alex returned a few minutes later with a meatball sub and a cup of soda, deciding after one bite that a bit of game time would be more enjoyable than just eating; the sole remaining character sheet, a sorcerer this time, was his as soon as Trevor gave him to go-ahead to join. "I've got the gist of the gameplay, but where are we?"

"Searching a nearby graveyard," said the player to his left, to which Alex smiled to himself.

"No sign of anything?"

"Nothing visible, but..."

Alex nodded. "Then, I start looking around, seeing if anything magical grabs me."

"Which direction?" Trevor asked.

"Towards the biggest structure nearby, I guess."

"That would be a mausoleum on the northeast side."

"Then I head that way, in search of magical corruption or the like."

The front doorbell chimed as Trevor spoke, taking Alex's attention away briefly. "As you approach, you feel something akin to disgust run up your arms, something that feels immune to being washed away."

"That's it," said one of the players.

"Let's hope. I call out to all of you."

Between the players saying they were getting into position, Alex heard the register open, followed by rustling that he knew from trading card package foil. *Must've had a big sale.* It was a few seconds later when an uncomfortable feeling washed over him. The register wasn't being closed; Marcus was fast with that.

"On second thought, excuse me a second." Alex didn't wait for a response before slipping out of the room. Although hoping it was nothing, as soon as he had a view of the front, and of the register, his attention was locked on the hoodied thief holding up his friend, and the solid black pistol in his hand.

Chapter 20 ✦ Effective Violence

Saturday, October 22nd, 2011
Moon Phase – Waning Crescent

The warmth in Alex's skin vanished, and his heartrate shot up at the sight. He lowered himself into a stalking gait in turn, setting his shoes down softly with each step around the back, and then towards the thief. Though Marcus noticed him, within a second he glanced down again, resuming taking handfuls of the trading card packs and handing them onto the counter.

Motherfucker, Alex snarled to himself. Letting his gaze break for only a moment, he took the heaviest thing he could see into his hand. A book was a shit weapon, but one good smack to the head...

The thief then started reaching for the duffel bag on the counter, and knowing what that meant, Alex closed in. With no sound, he swung the book with both hands, spine first, when he felt close enough. The *thunk* it made was muffled by the hoodie's material, but the action rocketed his pulse even higher.

As the thief stumbled and grabbed the counter, uttering a pained swear in turn, Alex slammed the book into his head again, then tossed it and focused on the gun, grabbing it by the slide, near the trigger guard, and by the back, over the hammer.

The thought of biting the thief's arm to make him lose his grip barely crossed Alex's mind before he noticed him swing for his head and ducked. He then yanked at the weapon with the hand he had on the slide, only for the thief to take advantage of his hands being full and land a punch against his stomach.

Alex let out only an exhale at first, but then came another strike, this one to his head. The pain and sudden headache from the strike loosened his grip before he thrust his left elbow back. It hit something, what he couldn't tell, so he wound up for another.

It was when the second attack hit that Alex heard the clink from the pistol's hammer striking the firing pin.

No boom of gunpowder sounded, something that should've been a relief all-around. Alex however snarled openly, grabbed the weapon again, and this time pulled it up and back until the audible crunching of bone and tissue reached his ears.

With the thief's first pained scream, Alex made a fist with his right hand and swung with everything he had. The punch hit the thief square above his eye and staggered him. It was then that Alex felt the thief's grip give and he pulled the gun free. Refusing to relent, he shoved the thief with the whole of his body, forcing a loss of footing and a fall, giving him the time he needed to get the pistol into his grip and then press his shoe against the thief's face and neck.

"Motherfucker. Stay down!" Alex's breathing was ragged by that point, his snarling escaping his notice until he heard Marcus telling him to calm down, and that he was getting the police. Though Alex only glanced at him, the fear in his friend's eyes quickly jabbed a spear of cold into his heart.

No fangs. No claws either. His heartrate wasn't slowing down though, and now he could smell blood; his fingers were stained red after one swipe of the area where he'd been punched in the face.

Then came the voices behind him: Trevor and the other players. Unwilling to turn around, Alex held his foot in place and ejected the pistol's magazine. The sole 'bullet' inside was an aluminum snap-cap round, and when the slide was drawn back, another was ejected onto the glass countertop---something that did bring him some relief to see, although didn't wipe away his anger at what had just happened.

As the next minute inched by, Marcus remained on the phone with dispatch, detailing the scene, while Trevor tried to ease some words out of Alex, mostly regarding wellness questions. "Yeah, son of a bitch didn't get me too bad," Alex said before increasing the weight behind his planted shoe.

"Marcus, keep close to him." Trevor then said, waiting until he was out from behind the counter and by Alex's side before heading for the office.

In turn, Marcus got as good a look as he could at Alex's face. "He's bleeding a bit, near the eyebrow... Yes, he is... I can't tell. It sounded bad... Will do. Thanks." His next words went towards his friend. "Got a cruiser and an ambulance incoming."

"Good." Alex then turned his stare towards the thief. He was still whimpering, and mostly massaging the part of his hand that was broken.

"You alright?"

Alex licked his teeth again---still no fangs. He nodded.

By the time the police arrived---four in all between two cruisers---Trevor had returned with a baseball bat and taken up a spot near the door. With Alex keeping his attention and head downward, when his boss told him the police had arrived, he released his foot from the thief and stepped back; he'd handed the pistol and magazine to Marcus by then, leaving him to show that it wasn't loaded when they entered and saw him holding it.

It was when Alex looked ahead, readying to vouch for him, that his father came into view. Though his expression was mostly relief, the rest was general unease, a bit of which bled over into Alex.

"We'll take those," said one of the officers before Marcus handed over the pistol and magazine.

As the officer looked the weapon over, Alex's father told him to secure it, and then turned his attention to his son. "He's alright, Mr. Stryker," Marcus said.

"And you?"

"Shaken, and kind of angry, but alright."

After Alex's father nodded, he started looking around the scene. Alex was more focused on the ambulance that had just pulled up, their flashing lights adding to the annoyance his eyes felt. Shane's father wasn't among the duo that emerged from the ambulance, though he could already see him hearing word of this.

As the thief was assessed, Alex took the downtime to try and relax some more. Catching Marcus, Trevor, and two of the other players in glances, there was an even split between looks of impression and those of concern, the latter coming from Marcus and Trevor. Returning the impressed looks of the players as the thief was carted outside, the three remaining police officers started picking out someone to ask questions about the incident.

"You first," Alex's father said to him, to which Marcus gave him a nod and stepped aside. After being escorted a short distance, his father continued. "You okay?"

Alex exhaled before he spoke. He knew his father wouldn't buy a simple nod, and already he was starting to tremble. "Mostly."

"Take a minute and calm down if you need to." His father then placed a hand on his shoulder as Alex closed his eyes. "That cut needs looking at."

"It'll heal. Quick."

"Still, just sit through the basic part, Son. Alright?"

Alex nodded, and as he reopened his eyes, spotted one of the EMTs coming his way, asking if he was ready to be examined. Though tempted to ask how much damage he'd done to the thief's wrist, he kept quiet as the EMT did his job.

"Looks like the bleeding already stopped," the EMT said after dabbing the cut. "Hmm… Doesn't look like it'll need any stitches."

"Just what I wanted to hear," Alex said with a weak smile.

"What about your chest? Any pain? Discomfort?"

Alex felt the spot where he'd been punched. "No."

"Then, just keep that cut clean and you should be fine."

"Will do. Thanks." Alex gave the EMT a fist-bump before he started heading back to the ambulance, after which his father resumed speaking, going through the range of questions typical of an attempted robbery, each part noted in his notebook. Aside from one: "Did you notice anything change?"

Alex was certain his eyes had, but that was ignorable. After he shook his head, his father followed up with, "Good. Can't tell you how glad I am that you didn't get shot or end up changing in here."

Though unwilling to argue, Alex refused to think his decision to help his friend, however violent it turned out, was anything besides just. Sneaking a look in Marcus's direction, he was paying more attention to the officer speaking to him. Trevor was doing the same, with the duffle bag's contents emptied out onto the counter, likely for photographing and logging by the police.

"So, now what?" Alex asked after a bit.

"That's up to your boss. Otherwise, it's better that we not leave your mother out of the loop about this."

Alex silently accepted, and until the police left half an hour later, he was left wondering and fearing what his boss would now see in him. As he and Marcus replaced the near-stolen trading cards and bills a while later, he kept sneaking glances at Trevor, watching for hints of unease.

As it happened, his boss didn't approach him until he was about to clock out. Alex saw no hints of unease in his expression, nor heard any within the first few words his boss said to him, which boiled down to if he needed to leave right away. "Good," Trevor said after Alex replied that he didn't. "Just wanted to thank you for stopping that thief."

"Oh…" Alex stumbled on his words for a moment, tossing a few replies aside before settling on, "No problem. Never thought I'd see that here."

"It's happened before, years ago. That aside, I overheard the EMT give you a clean bill of health. Just in case, are you certain everything's fine?"

"Yeah, just…" Alex pointed to his left eyebrow.

"I can relate; it happened to me once. Anyway, good to know. I'll see you on Monday."

"You too, boss," Alex said, meeting his boss's hand with a firm shake.

Back at home, the good vibes that had built from Trevor's short talk with him served as fresh mental armor when his mother was given the news. Shock and overwhelming gratitude soon pushed her into giving Alex a lengthy hug, her fear scent flooding his nostrils in turn.

"That was very brave of you, Alex, but you should've considered the chance that you might have been hurt much worse," his father said as his mother kept hugging him.

Figuring his father was implying what might have happened if the pistol had live rounds, for some reason, Shane's words snuck back into his head. About the blood on his skin and why he'd been bitten. It took a few more seconds for a chill to pierce his skin. If he had been shot… *Damn it, no. Nothing happened, and the EMT was wearing rubber gloves.*

After his mother stopped hugging him and dinner was over, Alex settled back into his room to game for a while. Nothing really bad had happened. He had no reason to focus on the negatives.

Sunday, October 23rd, 2011
Moon Phase – Waning Crescent

The next day, after looking and sniffing around the wooded area across the street, Alex eased Bailey south into the neighborhood. A walk to, and then back from Nathan's house felt long enough for the day, even with the dipping temperatures contrasting the exposed sunlight.

Once there, Alex readied Bailey's portable drinking bowl and rubbed his head as he lapped the water from it. With the direction of the breezes, he couldn't smell Ginger or anything else from his friend's house, but on the way back, after branching off from the route he initially followed, he noticed what he was certain was Shane's scent. Figuring he was waiting for a reason to approach the house, and him, Alex reversed course, taking his original route north.

As he took his first steps in the grass leading up to the bundle of trees, Shane emerged from behind the left line of fences and gestured for him to come, moving further back into the area afterward. Once he'd stopped and Alex was close enough, Shane began with, "So, what did your parents think?"

"Of?"

"The offer my dad made you. What else?"

Alex broke eye contact with a reluctant sigh. "Haven't told them yet."

"Or that you met us, I bet."

"No. They think I gave your dad a 'Thank You' note."

"You kinda did by visiting. You're not something we need to worry about anymore."

"Then what was that fuss about me being 'dependent' about?" Shane didn't immediately answer; Alex refrained from the first remark he wanted to make, as well as the second, and the third.

"If for some reason they don't like the idea, say something like my dad insists or something."

"No, I'll just tell them the truth."

"Suit yourself, but if that doesn't work, just come anyway." Shane then turned his attention to Bailey, urging Alex to rub his head. "While I'm here," he said after some silence, "who saw you attack that thief?"

Figures. "Marcus...and my boss. Why?"

"Just curious."

"Nothing visibly changed."

"Then you dealt with whoever that was quickly enough, or you knew you had the advantage. Either way, be thankful."

Alex refrained from saying that he was, even though what concerns he had in relation to the incident were minute at best.

Chapter 21 – Straightening the Record

Sunday, October 23rd, 2011
Moon Phase – Waning Crescent

As After Shane departed a few minutes later, Alex pulled out his phone and held it for a moment. Had Marcus already told Catherine and Nathan about what happened? As he wondered, something akin to a warm flash went through him. Yeah, he'd broken someone's wrist, but not without good reason. They'd see that, surely, and they'd already seen him as a werewolf.

But then, he hadn't seen, or gotten a text or call from Catherine in awhile. *She can't be nervous still, can she?* As Shane's words about his friends trying not to be scared of him worked their way back into his head, Alex sent her a short text, hoping she would respond and quell the concern he was now harboring.

An hour went by without a response, and then two. *Maybe she's busy.* After that thought, he fired off a text a piece to both Marcus and Nathan, asking if they had a few minutes.

Marcus responded first.

Marcus A.: Yeah.

> *Alex S.:* I haven't heard from Catherine in a while. Everything okay?

Marcus A.: As far as I know.

> *Alex S.:* Alright. Just a bit concerned, that's all.

What Marcus said next left several emotions pulling at Alex's thoughts.

Marcus A.: I told her about the attempted robbery.
She doesn't know you stopped the guy, or how.

At first, Alex could see the logic; telling her he'd broken someone's wrist likely wouldn't endear her to him very much. And then there was what his dad had said, about potentially getting hurt worse, or shot. But she wasn't the type to misplace, or simply fling, blame.

Alex S.: Mind if I ask what you did tell her?

Marcus A.: It's alright, man. I don't want her to
worry about what happened.

Alex S.: I get you.

Marcus A.: If she asks, you saw the guy and
then he bolted. Can you do that?

Alex sighed as he typed out his response.

Alex S.: No problem.

Marcus A.: Thanks.

When Nathan later responded that he had just gone on break, hence the delay, Alex told him he'd already spoken to Marcus, but thanks anyway.

* * *

Better get this over with, Alex thought to himself as he got up from the dinner table for seconds. His folks had yet to bring up anything related to where he could get animal meat, something that gave him a touch of confidence about being able to convince them of the offer he'd accepted.

He started the line of questions as soon as his plate was full. "Dad?" His father hummed in response. "Any of the officers have any suggestions?"

"About...oh. Beyond buying what you'd need from a butcher, no."

"Okay," Alex responded, trying to stay tone neutral.

"What about you?" his mother asked.

"I think I found something." Alex felt his pulse increase as he spoke.

"Really? What is it?"

Alex took in a silent, deep breath. "Remember how Shane brought that meat before?"

Though his mother was first to reply, his father didn't wait to express what he felt. "I thought you wanted nothing to do with him."

"I can tolerate him."

"Even if that's what you think, what makes you think he'll help you?"

Alex clenched a hand under the table. "Because it's his dad who made me an offer, not him." The drop in his skin temperature felt like a mirror to how cold the room suddenly felt.

After his parents glanced at each other, his father went first. "When? And how?"

"A few days ago. That was what Shane wanted me over for."

"You visited them?" his mother asked. Alex barely noticed how wide her eyes were and could only nod.

"You said you didn't," his father said.

"It was to get this guy off my back."

"Regardless, Son, we told you not to."

"I know."

The talks stopped for a few seconds, and Alex took the initiative this time. "His dad's concerned, so he made me an offer."

"Concerned? About what?" his mother asked.

"The canine units."

Alex's father spoke next. "He's thinking they'll be led to where they live, right?"

Alex nodded.

"I thought so, but that's their problem, not yours."

"To a point. I'll have to go after something eventually."

"Not if you find a meat delivery service. You've got a few weeks to spare."

"Yeah, but what I got from Shane did the job. If what I pick doesn't work out, I'm screwed."

Things went silent again, and Alex again took the initiative.

"Maybe I can figure out where he gets his meat, and then buy my own after this coming full moon."

"He didn't tell you when you spoke to him?"

Alex shook his head. "I never asked."

"Why not?" his mother asked.

"I was nervous," Alex said after a brief exhale.

"I can't imagine why," his father said.

"What made you nervous?" his mother asked.

"I didn't know what his parents were like, or what I could afford to say."

"And what were they like?"

"Pretty nice, and soft-spoken, I guess."

His father hummed again. "What did they offer you?"

"Enough to feed me when I need it, possibly a bit more."

"For what, or how much?"

"Seventy-five."

Once again his mother's eyes widened, though not as much as before. His father kept quiet, his gestures making it clear he was thinking over what was just said.

"It's not cheap, I know, but the slab Shane gave me was at least seven pounds, and I had some left over."

"That's all they want?"

For a moment, Alex questioned whether to mention anything else. "I'll need to get over there at some point, but that's it."

"'Get over there'?" his mother asked.

"Sneak over to his house, before I get hungry."

"But you just said the canine units were a worry."

"Not if I go over there really late at night, or early in the morning, and be extremely careful."

"Did you already agree to all of this?" his father asked.

"I haven't paid them yet."

"Then I'd say go with what you suggested before: find out where they got what they gave you and see if you can buy from them yourself."

"Alright." In the back of his mind, Alex felt a niggling doubt that it would be as easy as that.

Wednesday, October 26th, 2011
Moon Phase - New

The three days leading up to his next payday gave Alex enough time to think about things, including what to ask of Shane's parents. His friends were back in mind as soon as Monday came, however. Nathan had heard about the attempted robbery incident thanks to Catherine, but as a reaffirmation of what Marcus had told him, only an abridged version had reached him.

And Alex couldn't help asking, "Did Marcus bring it up at all?"

"No, just Catherine," Nathan said as they headed towards the stairwells. The uncomfortable feelings Alex got from that answer didn't have long to worsen before his friend continued. "Now that you mention it, that is weird."

They were halfway down the first stairwell when Alex decided to say something. "When did she tell you?"

"Yesterday."

"Hmm. You've only heard half the story, then."

"What's the other half?"

Alex glanced around before answering. "That thief didn't get away. I fought him and did a number on his wrist."

This time, Nathan spoke after a delay. "Seriously?" Alex nodded. "Now I'm confused."

"Marcus told me he didn't want Catherine to worry…" At that, something clicked. "Did she mention a weapon at all?"

"Just that the guy claimed to have one."

"Oh," Alex said, drawing out the word. "That explains it. He left out the weapon and what I did."

"Can't say I see a reason for it, but thanks for filling me in."

"No problem, man." The shift at Blue Moon that followed saw Alex working without Marcus around.

* * *

Once his class was over on Wednesday, and a single hour of skating at the Tampa shop was behind him, Alex gathered his paycheck from Trevor and cashed it, tucking the seventy-five he needed into the watch pocket of his jeans. The idea of returning to Shane's house still made his skin tighten, even after a short walk with Bailey.

In the end, it was approaching 3:30 p.m. when he pulled up to the curb in front of the house. The Jeep he'd seen before was there, but not the SUV.

As he began to question coming back later, the front door opened, revealing Shane. The eastbound breezes kept him from catching the scents the open door was letting loose, keeping his unease down.

"It's just me and Dad if you're coming in," Shane said when he was within a few feet.

I figured. "In a minute," Alex said as his motorcycle's engine was shut off.

"I'll leave the door unlocked, then." As Shane walked away, Alex checked his phone and backpack, only removing his helmet when he was halfway up the walkway to the door. Inside, their scents put him further on the defensive, delaying his response to Shane's father asking if that was him.

"You thirsty, or do you have some water with you?" he asked, likely from the kitchen.

"I've got some," Alex answered. In response, he noticed Shane's father appear in the doorway to his right, past the showcase dining area.

Instead of coming any closer, he leaned against the doorframe. "Still nervous?"

Alex glanced away instead of answering, but the silence he was met with was hint enough that Shane's father wanted him to answer. "Yeah," he finally said.

"Then, while you're here, how about Shane and I show you around and answer any other questions you've got?"

Shane appeared out of the corner of Alex's eye as he considered the suggestion. He couldn't see such a thing helping after he'd left the house, and felt almost certain both Shane and his father knew it. But then, he soon thought, he wouldn't need to stay in their house all day, if that.

"Sure," was the answer Alex soon gave, to which Shane's father nodded.

"Shane?" Once he responded, his father continued. "Let's show him around first."

Chapter 22 – Ask And Receive

Wednesday, October 26th, 2011
Moon Phase - New

Alex second-guessed his answer for a few seconds after hearing that. Shane's forceful stare soon broke him away from where he felt safest, and he followed them toward the hallway on the left side of the living room.

"Since you'll be here for a while, there's an empty guest room you can stay and change back in," Shane's father said, gesturing towards the room that, by location, was closest to the front of the house. Though the door was closed, Alex recalled some kind of blinds blocking outside views in.

"Not a hundred percent empty," Shane stated after a moment.

"No, but empty enough. Here." Alex watched from a distance as the door was opened, revealing a wooden armoire, a rolled-up rug, and musty looking brown carpet. An onrush of air by his face confirmed the last part. "It smells funny in there, I know, but you'll have the space to change back when that time comes."

After the door was closed again, Shane's father gestured towards another room, one where Shane was leaning on the door. "That's his room." Alex immediately pictured Shane sneaking out of his room the same way he had before, and some of the things he'd potentially brought back. "Ours is down there, and the bathroom's right next to you."

Alex nodded.

"Now, just in case this has crossed your mind, when it comes to the meat we get, we don't get it until the very day we need it." Alex raised an eyebrow at that. "There is a reason for that, that being it ensures there's no risk of us being left hungry."

"You want to know why I got on you before? That's why," Shane said.

"I don't quite…"

Shane's father took over. "The sooner you deal with that hunger, the less you'll need in the end."

"See?" Shane added.

Sensing the smugness in Shane's tone, Alex replied, "I wouldn't have eaten Bailey or my family."

"Alex, please. Shane, don't." Shane's father then waited a few seconds. "It's not about whether you would or would not do something like that. You very easily could, as could Shane or I, so every chance you get, keep yourself from doing it."

Alex felt a question form, but didn't act on it.

"On that, how did you lose your last catch?"

After a glance at Shane's father, then at Shane himself, who simply thrust a hand out, Alex answered. "Its hooves kept striking my wrists."

"I see."

"And the police being right there...I couldn't help it. I panicked."

"I don't blame you." Shane's father turned his attention towards his son for a moment, his expression shifting to disappointment.

"How was I to know it would bother him that much?" Shane retorted.

Instead of verbally responding to his son, Shane's father gave a lengthy sigh, and then returned his attention to Alex. "What was it about the animal that made you hesitate?"

Alex felt his pulse rise a few beats as he thought back to why. "The whole thing."

"No specifics?"

Alex shook his head. "Too many things about it."

"Hmm." Shane's father rubbed his chin for a moment. "I know this may not sound reasonable, but have you hunted before, with a gun?"

Not reasonable? "Once, years ago."

"Okay. I ask because the animals you hunt will always make noise, but if you've hunted and feel more comfortable with a weapon..." Shane's father paused.

"Carry a gun while I'm a werewolf?" Although Alex now understood what Shane's father had meant, when he gave the idea a few seconds to stew, he began seeing merits to the idea.

"We can just as easily show him how to do it right," Shane said.

"Given what he's told you, not for a while."

"How long could that be?" Alex asked.

"To be frank, I don't know. I've never had to deal with canine police, and I doubt you're in any position to get information concerning their length of need."

For a moment, Alex saw an opportunity, but Shane jumped in before he could act on it. "Dad, he shouldn't be dependent on us."

Alex silently told Shane to stuff it before realizing his opportunity hadn't been lost. "If it bothers you, I could always buy my own meat, the same way you do."

Shane's father was quick to respond. "No, you couldn't." When Alex looked toward him again, eyebrows raised, he continued. "I get the meat my son and I need through a longtime friend of mine. I know his supply works for us, but I had to figure out the circumstances to ensure that, and talk him into helping us. You don't want to juggle trying to figure out all of that this close to the full moon, especially with what you told my son."

"Then, can you help me get a handle on this?"

"As best I can, but not right now."

Damn it.

"My son means well, trust me."

He hasn't proven it very well, though.

"But I wouldn't call this circumstance dependency, by any stretch. For now, we have to stay quiet and let things die down." His gaze shifted to Shane. "And this is the best way to do it."

Alex snuck a look at Shane, who seemed unmoved by his father's implications, before speaking again. "Have there been issues?"

"Yes, many."

Despite the implication of those words, the quick and oddly even-toned response from Shane's father relaxed Alex's nerves a bit.

"There's always a chance of it, and Shane and I have had to do last-minute hunts in the past because of them."

"Meaning several years ago," Shane said as his father paused.

Alex strained in vain to recall anything from during high school that sounded like a werewolf could've been responsible as Shane's father resumed. "Yes. We haven't had any such issues for a long while, and shouldn't have any this time."

If that's true... Alex could feel his next sentence taking form, but questioned if now was the best time to ask. Another glance at Shane told him it wasn't.

"Speaking of issues, how did your folks respond?" Shane asked.

"Begrudgingly," Alex said, his gaze not trained on either Shane or his father.

"I'm not surprised."

"Even so," Shane's father began, "you're here, so I think they understood enough."

Alex felt his watch pocket at that, ready to hand over the money he needed. "Mmm. They really want me to find an alternative of some kind, though."

"To us?" Shane asked.

"To that animal hunger," Alex said.

Things went quiet for a moment. "I can sympathize," Shane's father said, "but, from experience, there isn't one."

Alex sighed quietly at that.

"That you want to consider," Shane added, to which his father hummed.

"That's not an admission of defeat, just of what it is."

Alex didn't respond. The forming lump in his throat wouldn't let him.

"If it helps, look at it this way: it's a once-a-month situation that you can plan around, and if you're not keen on killing with your own hands, the meat you'll receive from us gets around that as well."

"Yeah," Alex said after a delay and a breath. Neither Shane nor his father made an attempt to push him to speak, even after he produced the seventy-five dollars from his watch pocket and handed it over.

"The realization wasn't pleasant for me either," Shane's father said, "but I grew used to it, and this setup has helped us a lot in the end."

As Alex began wondering how many homes Shane's family had been in and out of up to now, another part of him was readying to bring what he was told to his folks, and being torn on how they would react. Shane's father then offered him a drink, which he refused in favor of the one he'd brought; Bailey's scent from the air in his pack helped quell some of the lump in his throat.

* * *

That night, Alex didn't wait for dinner before speaking up. Judging strictly from the initial expressions of his folks, he was correct on at least one assumption: his father was begrudged by the news. "How certain are you that what they told you was true?" he asked.

"Very," Alex said. "The slab Shane gave me was still warm, like it had been freshly cut."

As his father sighed and propped his forehead against a free hand, his mother spoke. "They're not going to have any issues with that, are they?"

Alex shook his head. "They shouldn't."

"What if they do?"

"Then we'll have to wait an extra hour or so." When his folks stayed quiet, Alex continued. "If that wasn't reliable, their house wouldn't be so lived-in."

"How could you tell that?"

"It smelled like it, among other things."

"Are they willing to let you buy meat from them beyond this one time?"

"Yeah."

"You're sure?"

Alex nodded. "That was what I was told before." His parents then exchanged glances instead of saying a word.

"Do you trust them with that?" his father asked.

"So far."

Another pause. "Then if you feel that's the best option, keep your mother and I up to date on things, and your options open."

At that, Alex's mother closed the distance and hugged him, his father doing the same only once she'd let go of him. "I will."

Chapter 23 – The Right Choice?

Friday, October 28th, 2011
Moon Phase – Waxing Crescent

"Any updates on the meat situation?" Nathan asked as their class was preparing to start.

Alex glanced around before answering. "I think so, but I'll tell you later." At that, his friend nodded and returned to his homework pile.

Throughout the class, Alex was torn on what to tell him. The supplier line would be the easiest, but if he lied and his friend figured out it was really Shane's family supplying him... Alex began leaning towards a two-sided answer as the last five minutes of class arrived, and once he and Nathan were far enough away from the room, he coaxed him aside.

"Yeah," Alex began. "Made some progress on it."

"Good to hear."

"For the moment, I've got one supplier in mind. Should work."

"They have good prices?"

Alex shrugged. "I guess. Wish they had some variety, though."

"Can't say I relate, but okay."

"There is another option, though."

"Which is?"

Alex watched his friend's reaction closely as he spoke. "Shane's family. Let them supply me."

Nathan's expression didn't cross into shock as Alex had been expecting. Instead, he let out a sigh. "They talked to you about that?"

"Brought it up, yeah. They're willing to do it, so long as I can pay for it."

Nathan hummed in response.

"Shane wasn't thrilled with the idea."

This time, Nathan's eyebrows scrunched a bit. "That's...kind of stupid. Why?"

"I don't know. Pride, maybe." When his friend didn't respond, Alex continued, by then having reconsidered his words. "Or maybe not. He sounded...like he was certain it was a bad idea."

"I wouldn't consider keeping safe a bad idea."

"Me either," Alex said before recalling his question about complications with getting meat. *He said several years ago that day... Did Angela have any part in that?*

Alex's musings were interrupted by Nathan speaking up. "Anyway, if his folks are offering..."

"I'm keeping them in mind."

"Good." Nathan paused for a moment to check the time, remarking right after that he needed to leave. Alex followed him until they reached the first floor, all the while glad that his friend wasn't too apprehensive about the deal he'd already accepted.

Once at work, Marcus's presence immediately nagged him. Would he and Catherine have similar feelings about the arrangement? Though Shane's statement about keeping things to himself came back to mind, Nathan already knew the possibility was there. How likely was he to spread word of that to Catherine or Marcus?

In the end, Alex waited until his friend was close to leaving for the night before approaching him and bringing up the subject. Like Nathan, he seemed pleased by the news of a "supplier", but at the mention of Shane's offer, his tone changed.

"Hang on a second. If he's offering that to you... Why didn't he do that before the first time this happened?"

When Alex struggled to come up with a solid answer, Marcus sighed and continued.

"Let me guess. He kept quiet about what he did to you?"

Alex shook his head after a second.

"Then, I still don't get why they waited until now to even consider this."

"Me either," Alex said before correcting himself a second later. "Or, no, scratch that. Shane kept telling his folks I was doing fine."

"I'm curious how he got that impression," Marcus said with a miffed angle to his tone.

"He probably lied. His dad didn't sound pleased that he'd bitten me, even with the excuse he gave."

"That you got her blood on you that night?"

Alex nodded.

"Yeah, even if his reasoning was sound, he... Gah."

Alex spoke up after a few moments of silence. "For the long term, I think that offer is my best bet."

"I'd still keep that other supplier in mind, though. At least as a way to stop depending on them if they start demanding too much of you."

Alex felt a touch of cold at Marcus's use of "depending". "I'll do that. Thanks, man."

Saturday, October 29th, 2011
Moon Phase – Waxing Crescent

I'm not depending on them. I've already hunted twice, and they offered, Alex told himself as the afternoon approached the next day. Despite that self-assurance, his friend's statement kept prodding at his brain. The situation around town was the way it was because of Shane, and now his family was going to be the source of what he needed to keep safe from harm and engaging in cannibalism. When Bailey settled into a rest over his legs, Alex stroked his head and back and leaned against the foot of his bed.

But still it nagged at him. Most of the kills had come after he'd been bitten, not before, and he still had no idea what had pushed Shane to do all of that when his family had their own food source. One theory soon came to mind, but he couldn't see a lick of sense in them risking their livelihoods just to pressure him into siding with them for easy meat. Much less when they were just as at risk as he was of getting spotted or tracked.

Even so, once Bailey removed himself from his position atop his legs, Alex made for and powered on his computer. His first fifteen minutes of searching turned up several places that could supply meat, but none that offered fresh cuts of several pounds for less than a hundred dollars. *Whoever Shane's dad knows, he's gotta live close to here if that meat comes to them warm.*

The sound of his phone ringing a few minutes later caused him to jump in his seat. *Who's calling me?* he thought after seeing the unnamed number. The first ring went by unanswered, as did the second. The third ring was when he answered.

"Hello?"

"Good, it's you."

Shane's voice sent a chill through his back. *The hell...* "How'd you get this number?"

"Just listen for a second and don't hang up on me, alright?"

"Why shouldn't I?"

"Because I don't want to have to watch out for you on Monday, that's why."

Watch out for me on Monday? "What's that got to do with anything?"

"At this point, nothing, unless you make it something."

Son of a… When Alex checked his desktop's calendar, he was quickly reminded that that day was Halloween. *What's his point?*

After echoing the question verbally, Shane responded, "Just give me your assurance that you won't do anything stupid that night."

"If you stop beating around the bush and tell me what that's supposed to mean."

"I want your promise that you won't shift and go around freaking people out that night."

Alex's anger laxed for a moment once things were made clear. Was that something Shane had seen another werewolf do and get hurt for? Or was it something he'd once done? His father didn't seem like the type to let something like that slide if he found out.

"What gave you the impression that I would even think of doing that?"

"You've shifted on your own twice already, and a night like that would mean less suspicion, unless the canine cops showed up."

"It's not like I wanted to shift last time."

"Then what prompted you the first time?"

At first, Alex didn't want to respond, thinking that his answer would validate Shane's concerns, but when he asked himself how Shane knew he'd shifted twice on his own, he was torn between the image of being watched and his scent giving it away.

"Concern, for one thing." Alex eventually said. "Didn't work like I wanted, but at least I know something because of that."

"Fair enough."

At least you've got some sense. "Why so much concern about that day, though?"

"Just being safe."

"Or you saw Angela doing that and thought I would too."

"No, and if she ever did, she never said a thing about it to me or Dad."

Alex didn't follow up.

"Whatever. So long as you're not lying to me."

"I'm not."

Shane waited a few seconds to respond. "Then I'll believe you. One more thing: don't block this number. It's my dad's. He'll call you if we need to tell you something."

"Fine, then." A second later, Alex heard the click signaling the other phone hanging up. *Thanks for the chastising, asshole.*

As he set his phone aside, Alex went back to thinking about other reasons why Shane would be concerned about him shifting. After some time, the only thing he could conclude was a lack of food.

That would make sense... Wait a minute, is the school's stable really empty? After applying the same question to the ranch they'd hit last time, Alex headed outside and to his motorcycle. The breezes were coming from the north, but even when he drove down the road directly south of his high school, he couldn't smell the animals.

What he found when he arrived and walked close to the stable was proof Shane hadn't been lying. The doe's enclosure was cleaned of blood, as he expected, but every other section had only faint scent traces of the animals once housed inside.

The ranch was another story. While pretending to use his phone for something, Alex noticed barbed wire surrounding a few pens and fresh metallic fencing in spots. He couldn't hear any crackling or humming in line with electricity but couldn't see another reason for that kind of fencing and drove off.

On the drive home, he couldn't help wondering how different things would've been if Shane hadn't gone on his killing spree, and then how long he would've had before his options for food became strained.

Chapter 24 - A Cautious Halloween

Monday, October 31st, 2011
Moon Phase - Waxing Crescent

How Shane, or his father, had gotten their hands on his phone number remained on Alex's thoughts into Sunday morning. He hadn't filled out any medical or contact paperwork after the fight at work, nor had he seen Shane's father in any of the places he'd been over the last week. He couldn't remember noticing his scent either, but with that, he remembered that his friends were watching for Shane, not his father.

As he pulled his phone out, he took a moment to think. Shane's family already had his number, and they knew where he lived. What would telling his friends, and potentially stressing them out as well, even accomplish at this point?

After a minute, he resolved to only tell them if they directly asked him about Shane and his family, and then saved the number into his phone.

Once Monday came, his mood perked up at Nathan's announcement of the next Mage session. "Friday will work for me," Alex said as class began, and throughout the following few hours, ideas of what could be next for the group came and went.

* * *

"No plans tonight?" Marcus asked as he and Alex were straightening the shelves of the shop.

Alex couldn't help remembering the phone call with Shane. "No. Figure I'll stay inside and play with Bailey. Or play a few games."

Marcus stayed quiet for a few moments. "Think your folks would mind if I came over?"

"They shouldn't. One of the officers Dad works with holds a party for the department every year, and he and Mom and going again."

"All night?"

"Usually."

"Then, how does six to nine sound? Catherine wants me to help her with something after my shift, and I've got some homework to finish up before tomorrow."

Alex held his initial answer off once Catherine was mentioned. "I still haven't heard a thing from her in a while."

"She's been busy. Family stuff."

How quickly his friend responded eased Alex's initial worries. "Nothing bad I hope."

"Not as far as I know. Anyway, I can spare those three hours if you'd like to hang out."

"Sure, and give Catherine my regards when you see her."

"Will do."

* * *

By the time Marcus arrived, Alex's parents had yet to leave. He'd spent some time beforehand keeping watch on the empty lot across the street. Nothing besides trick-or-treaters had passed by it so far, but a part of him expected Shane to ignore their discussion and watch the house anyway. So far the south-bound breezes hadn't confirmed he was nearby, but that still left the possibility that he was somewhere south of the house, waiting for something to react to.

Alex had also wrestled with the idea of texting Shane's father to confirm his suspicions. In the end, he didn't; for all he knew, Shane's father was on-shift for the night, and wouldn't know where his son was.

Marcus didn't wait until they were inside to raise a question. "Keeping an eye out for that guy?"

"Yeah. No sign of him, thankfully."

"No kidding."

Inside, Alex left Marcus to greet and talk to his folks for a bit while he got his friend a drink.

"So, are you guys going to hang around here, or..." his mother asked as he returned and offered the second glass.

"Yeah, I think so," Marcus replied, to which Alex nodded.

"In that case, just keep the porch lights off. We'll probably be home before midnight."

"Alright," Alex said before rubbing Bailey's head. Once his folks were gone, his attention flipped to what they could do for the next few hours.

Marcus had already suggested a bit of gaming. "I did bring my laptop with me," he'd said after Alex suggested setting up his XBOX into the living room. "Why don't we get some DOOM going?"

"Vanilla, or something modded?"

"Whatever, so long as it's deathmatch."

Alex smiled. "Works for me."

It didn't take long after the start of the first match for Alex to start feeling excited as opposed to cautious; his pulse rose as he and his friend exchanged fire and claimed frags from each other.

"Hey, I need a quick break," Marcus said after a quarter of an hour.

"Alright. I'm kinda hungry anyway," Alex said as he got up and made for the kitchen. While he fixed up a few things to snack on, he heard Marcus approach the kitchen, but not move beyond the dining area. "I've got plenty of food if you want something," Alex said.

"Maybe later. Thanks, though." Alex silently accepted, only for his friend to speak up again after a minute. "While we're not busy, I've been meaning to ask. Has this Shane kid pressured you in any way?"

Alex felt a chill at that question. "Recently, or..."

"Any time since the last full moon."

For a moment, Alex wondered if this was the real reason Marcus had chosen to come over. "Aside from getting me to meet his parents, no."

"Then, have you caught him skulking around the house? You did say you were watching for him."

Damn it. "No. He was worried that I'd use tonight to shift and cause mischief."

Marcus's response was a mostly of confusion. "What?"

"I know. That's the same way I reacted." Alex continued when his friend kept quiet. "He said he believed me when I told him I wasn't going to, and had no plans of the sort, but I couldn't shake the feeling he wanted to watch me anyway."

Marcus sighed loudly. "That sounds like pressuring to me. Unless he's willing to knock that off, I'd refuse what his family is offering."

"If he makes a habit of it, sure. I have other options. Still, when he brought that up, the whole thing felt more like baseless fears than anything else."

"How ironic. He accuses you of being paranoid, then acts the same way weeks later."

"It could be his family thinking that way instead of him, but if not, yeah."

"What makes you say that?"

Alex stopped himself from replying right away. "Just a feeling I got after talking to his dad. He seemed the most concerned about the possibility of trouble with the police."

"Can't say I'm surprised. What was he like, though?"

"Really relaxed and direct, most of the time. He only raised his voice when Shane and I started arguing. Hated how nervous that made me feel."

"He must be used to dealing with werewolves if that happened."

Alex debated saying Shane's father was also a werewolf. "Maybe. I was a guest at the time though, and they did feed me after I lost my catch."

Marcus hummed in response, and then kept quiet while Alex went back to snacking on his choice of foods. Only when his friend refilled his empty glass did he speak again. "So, if you had to make a choice, say, by tomorrow, would you get meat from them, or keep looking for a supplier?"

Alex stayed quiet until it felt like the right time to answer. A period of what felt like minutes, and the longer he stayed quiet, the tighter his chest got.

"Them," he eventually said. "If what I got myself was useless or I didn't get it in time, I'd have to hunt anyway, and the places I've used are tightening security or pulling the animals."

Marcus responded after a few seconds. "Can't say I blame you if that's the case."

Despite hearing no hint of concern in his friend's voice, Alex tried to assure him anyway. "Nathan offered to help, but I'd rather not get you guys involved. I'll keep looking for an alternative after this next full moon, and if I find one, I'll cut them off and that'll be that."

"Sounds good. Good luck with that, man."

Alex fist-bumped Marcus after noticing he'd held a fist up for him, and for the remainder of his friend's stay that night, the only things on their minds were the games they chose to play.

Chapter 25 - The First Move

Monday, October 31st, 2011
Moon Phase – Waxing Crescent

As the time arrived for his friend to leave that night, Alex slipped outside to check once again for any sign of Shane. The lot across the street was clear of any hint of him, though the breezes hadn't changed direction. He then checked the backyard. It was a stretch, since he'd heard plenty of noises from outside between moments of gaming, but Shane had already jumped the fence once.

The area behind the garage and the tops of the planks proved clean of his scent, and the dirt wasn't disturbed. If Shane had been observing him, he'd been smart enough to stay a good distance away.

Tuesday, November 1st, 2011
Moon Phase – Waxing Crescent

As he sat waiting for his second class to begin the next day, Alex heard his phone sound the IM tone. When he checked the message, despite it being so short he could read the whole thing without unlocking his phone, seeing Catherine as the sender sent a chill of surprise through him.

Catherine W.: Hey.

At first Alex was lost on what to say in response, but then his suspicions about Marcus's visit returned. Was what he told him the reason why she was texting him?

After a minute, Alex began typing.

Alex S.: Hey. Everything okay?

As he waited for her reply, he found it hard to fully focus on the novel in his hands. The tone came a few minutes later.

Catherine W.: Somewhat. Grandfather passed.

Oh... Yeah, that would keep her quiet for a while.

                                          Alex S.: Sorry to hear that.
                                          My condolences.

Catherine W.: Thanks.

Catherine's follow-up text took a minute to come in.

Catherine W.: Didn't mean to worry you.

Thought so.

                                          Alex S.: I had a feeling something
                                          was up. Was just hoping the cause
                                          wasn't me.

Catherine W.: No, and I appreciate you driving
off that thief.

Alex felt a twinge of guilt at the thought of continuing to hide the details
from his friend.

                                          Alex S.: Thanks. Wasn't about to
                                          let him get away with that.

No texts came after that.

                              * * *

Later that evening, as Alex's thoughts drifted to Shane and his family
again, he found himself recalling the plea he made last time—if his father
could help him with being a werewolf.

With his supposed phone number stored, he had a direct line to him... But what if he didn't want to talk over a phone because of the job he had? Or what if Shane had lied to him and the number was actually to his phone?

Alex held his phone for a while as the questions came and went. All he needed was one text to get things going. Just one...

After he began typing, he sat on the initial message for a minute, his mind tugging him between sending it and scrapping it. He didn't want to leave any hints of what he wanted until he was sure. Eventually he erased the text and rewrote it, hesitating for another minute before forcing himself to send it.

Alex S.: Do you have a minute?

Alex exhaled as he turned off his phone and set it aside. Nothing left to do besides...

His phone sounded the message tone less than five seconds later, making him jump a bit. Like Catherine's initial text, Alex could read it without unlocking his phone.

Shane's Dad: Is something wrong?

Why would he start with that? After a moment, Alex ignored that question and typed his response.

Alex S.: Just wanted to know, when could I talk to you? Without Shane around.

Shane's Dad: In person?

Alex S.: Yeah.

Shane's Dad: I'm assuming not in the house also.

Alex S.: If possible.

Shane's Dad: Well, I work full days from late morning to early evening, so it would have to be after I end my shift. Would Friday work? I know my son has plans that night.

Alex thought to Nathan's coming session after reading the message. The game had stopped at 8:30 last time...

Alex S.: If after 8:00 works.

The response he got after what felt like minutes relieved a bit of his worries.

Shane's Dad: It will. Do you know where you want to meet?

The seconds slipped past him as Alex tried to think of a good place. Before he could text back and say he wasn't sure, Shane's father continued.

Shane's Dad: Think it over, then text me the location.

Alex S.: Thanks.

Once his phone was set aside, Alex thought over his answer. Blue Moon wouldn't be busy that late at night, but if his boss was working, there was the risk that he would hear what was being said. For a moment Alex thought of meeting at Nathan's house, only to shake the idea out of his head. If Nathan was holding the game on-campus again, asking him to stay until Shane's father could come would achieve the same ends.

For a while, Alex couldn't see anything too wrong with the idea. The campus was a public place, with plenty of spots to talk that would be out of earshot of others. Plus, Nathan hadn't shown too extreme an emotion with anything related to Shane's family.

But then came his suspicions about how Nathan might react to such a request.

What if he accepted, then started demanding answers if he heard something that bothered him? How would Shane's father react to that? Alex tried to downplay the idea by reminding himself that it was Shane's fault this had happened, but then he remembered Angela. None of his friends knew her body had been stolen from the morgue that night.

No, he probably won't bring that up. Guilt twinged in Alex's stomach at that thought. Was it worth the risk? He'd handled Shane's family alone already, twice. Removing their house and Shane from the equation could only make things easier.

Another few minutes passed before he thought better of getting Nathan involved, and his phone was turned on again.

> *Alex S.*: How about the U of H campus near First Colony? I'll be there late that night.

Shane's father responded within a minute.

Shane's Dad: That works. I'll meet you there at 8.

Alex thanked him, then pocketed his phone.

Friday, November 3rd, 2011
Moon Phase - First Quarter
Time until the Shift - 6 Days, 12 Hours

By mid-afternoon Friday, Alex's gut had been tensing for the better part of an hour. He had several questions ready to go for when Shane's father came, but when he thought about the answers he might receive, the tension built a bit more.

A few easy breaths every so often barely helped, though he was glad Nathan had yet to notice anything. "One of the guys said he'll be a bit late," his friend said after putting his phone down. One of the other players nodded at the news while the rest kept their attention on their rulebooks, character sheets, or phones.

Alex, meanwhile, was trying to refocus on the game; they had stopped the previous game in the middle of an investigation. After a while, he slipped back into thinking more about the game and how he could assist the other players, though when attention was drawn to him, he could feel his mostly quelled anxiety start to resurface.

When a food break was called sometime later, Alex took the opportunity to slip away for a minute. His gut wasn't as tense anymore by then, but he still refrained from buying anything bigger than snack-sized.

Then came 6:30 p.m., when Nathan began to pull the session to a close. "Alright, so...you've all found the location where the stolen objects are being stashed." He took a moment to check his notes and write something down. "Anyone want to ready a spell, set up a ward, or anything else before we wrap things up?"

"Uh…" Alex began, stalling when he felt the other players focus on him. "I'll take point, watch for anyone coming."

"Me too," said the player sitting across from him. "Something tells me we're not completely safe here."

"Alright. Anything else?" Nathan waited a few seconds before continuing. "Then, we're done. Thanks for coming, everyone."

After replying in kind to his friend, Alex sat quietly and skimmed the changes to his character sheet. "Think I'll hang around the campus computer lab or something for a while before I leave," he said after all the other players had left.

"Alright. Later then," Nathan said before offering a hand to shake.

After his friend was out of sight, Alex headed upstairs to a find a quiet spot. Most of the campus was empty, save for the handful of evening classes, making it easy to find a spot where no noise would reach him. Once he'd found one, he settled down, took a few easy breaths, and spent a few minutes thinking about other things he could ask of Shane's father.

When he felt the tension returning, he took a breath and reminded himself that he'd meet this guy before. He knew what he was like at this point, and Shane wasn't a factor this time. So long as Shane's father answered what questions he had, put to rest what concerns he had left, that was all he cared about.

The last hour passed slower than he wanted, though it gave him the time to focus his thoughts. After gathering his stuff and readying his phone, Alex made for the closest stairwell and leaned against the railing.

What should I ask him first?

While he was deciding, he heard his phone sound the IM tone.

Shane's Dad: I'm here. Which building?

Chapter 26 — Past and Present

Friday, November 3rd, 2011
Moon Phase - First Quarter
Time until the Shift - 6 Days, 6 Hours

Alex went halfway down the stairway before he sent his response.

> *Alex S.*: The larger one, near the
> right-side parking lot.

Shane's Dad: I'll be there shortly.

Once downstairs, Alex headed for the east-end doors and watched through the glass. Within a minute, he spotted Shane's father heading his way, and his heartrate increased by a few beats. It stayed that way as he came inside, then built up more once he was standing within a few feet of him.

After Alex glanced up to match the green-eyed gaze of Shane's father, he noticed his attention move to his chest. *Damn it. Should've figured,* Alex thought as one hand curled some.

"Guess it can't be helped," Shane's father said after a moment. He then held out his hand.

It took Alex several seconds to grip it, but as soon as he did, the strength of the opposing hand became crystal clear.

"You have a spot picked out?" Shane's father asked after he stopped shaking Alex's hand.

Alex glanced aside. "Not really."

Shane's father glanced around some. Alex assumed he was getting an olfactory feel of the building.

"What about back there?" He pointed to the hallway Alex had just used.

"Uh, sure." Shane's father waited for him to move after that. He then matched his pace, and only once did he look aside.

When they reached the common area, Shane's father again did some glancing, as well as some small steps in certain directions. "Not the most private area," he soon said, "but if this is where you're comfortable, I'll accept."

Alex also took a glance around. The final classes of the day wouldn't let out until nine, and there were only a couple of people in the common area. He soon nodded and then led Shane's father to a spot near the windows.

After setting up a few things to make it look like they were there for some gaming rather than just talking, Alex took a moment to ready himself. Shane's father remained quiet, though his attention did waver every so often.

Alex's first words were preceded by an exhale. "What's Shane's problem with me?"

"He doesn't have a problem with you. It seems like it, I know, but that's because Shane's not like you or I."

Alex raised an eyebrow. "But he's a werewolf like you and me. What's different?"

"You and I were bitten. He wasn't," Shane's father continued before Alex could consider that for long. "He doesn't approach things the same way you or I do because he's never known what it's like to think strictly as a human."

Though Shane's father didn't elaborate past that statement, as Alex took his words into account, some of Shane's past behavior began to make more sense. At the same time, he felt a lump of sadness form in his chest. He could barely remember how it felt to not smell everything like a mosaic of scents, or to not have to look at crowds of people with a constant sense of suspicion and unease in his head.

Damn it. Not here, Alex thought as he fought back his emotions with a swallow and a sigh.

"I won't blame you if what he did upsets you, but I think you should know that he took what happened a lot less coldly than you might think."

As Alex recalled Nathan's statement about seeing Shane visibly upset in the past, he saw no recourse to argue. He did however have the opening he wanted to ask something else.

"Then, why'd he so suddenly go on an animal-killing spree after he bit me?"

This time, Shane's father took some seconds to answer. "I asked him the same question when I found out what he was doing. He said he felt hungry for some reason but wouldn't say anything else."

Sounds like an excuse to me.

"He's been quiet about it since then, but if that was true, then I'm glad he went after animals instead of someone on the street."

Though Alex was primed to respond as soon as Shane's father stopped talking, something about what was said made him hold off. Why would Shane have felt the hunger outside of the full moon, and so often? The only explanation he could see was he'd shifted for some reason and gotten hungry. But if that was what happened...

"That hunger, did it come when he was human?"

"Yes."

The fuck? Alex felt cold grip his heart. Was he also at risk of something like that?

As though sensing Alex's fear, Shane's father spoke up within a second. "I'm not certain, and I don't want to be, but I think it's because he tasted human blood and it set something off in him that I've never felt."

Alex remained silent as his memories were jogged. Though now he could see why Shane had been so on-edge when the hunger came up, why he'd beaten around the bush instead of outright telling him what could happen became the follow-up question.

Was it because he thought his statements alone were all that was needed? After a bit of time, that was the only conclusion Alex could draw.

"That was why I said before you should keep yourself as safe as possible."

Was that why he didn't wait to be sure? Recalling how intent Shane seemed on attacking him that night, even after his arm had been bitten into, Alex couldn't see another reason.

The silence between him and Shane's father lasted for several minutes after that. Nothing that entered his mind during that time pulled him too far into being upset or angry, but the other questions he wanted to ask became harder to focus on.

Eventually, he asked, "That Halloween call... Has he done that before?"

"No, he knows not to do that, even on a night like Halloween. I had a good feeling you wouldn't either, and I told him so, but he insisted we contact you and make sure."

Alex sighed. "So he was being a dick, like I thought."

"Yes, but that was as far as it went. As for how we got your number, I don't think that's important anymore. We needed a way to stay in contact with you, but I could tell you were too nervous to make a move on that."

Figures.

As Alex took a second to think about what to say next, a tone sounded from the phone Shane's father had. "It's my wife," he said after reading the message.

Figuring the message was in some way related to how much longer he would be away from home, Alex tried to pull his thoughts together as Shane's father typed out a reply. Once the phone was set aside, he took another breath, and then asked, "Did Shane tell you why he attacked Angela?"

Alex felt his skin grow cold after hearing those words leave his mouth, and Shane's father took a bit longer to respond.

"They didn't get along, that much I'm willing to say."

"I'm not asking to---"

"I know," Shane's father said, "but it's a sore subject with me and I'd rather not talk about it."

Alex swore he heard a slight shift in Shane's father's tone at those words, and refrained from sighing or acting disappointed, difficult as it was. "Alright. So, if Shane was born a werewolf--"

Shane's father spoke once Alex stalled. "I was worried about that for years myself, but Shane was born like anyone else was. He just grew a bit of fur on the next full moon, and that's when we knew. The lycanthropy never passed to my wife."

"So then, where did he get the blood-equals-infection idea from?"

"Me, and his health classes I'm sure. You worked at a vet before. I'm sure they told you not to allow direct skin contact with blood or other bodily fluids."

Alex nodded, then said, "So he was assuming."

"I would say so, but it was a fair one. That said, I won't be taking sides with you or my son on that. What's done is done; whose fault it is doesn't really matter anymore." When Alex looked aside and didn't respond, Shane's father took a breath. "I can spare a few more minutes to talk, if you need."

At that, Alex went with the first thing he could think of. "Question, then. I think my friends are figuring out you're supplying me. What should I do?"

"The best answer I can offer is try to reassure them. Tell them you thought over everything and, in the end, you went with us."

"Hope that's enough."

"You think it won't be?" Alex stalled on an answer, and Shane's father continued. "It's possible that could be the case, but if they're still talking to you, then honestly I think that chance is slim to none."

Alex sighed out his nose.

"If it helps, remember the friend of mine I mentioned when you last spoke to us?"

Alex nodded.

"He once saw me start to shift years ago, just like your friends did with you last month."

Alex swallowed and his pulse climbed a bit at those words. So Shane had told his father what happened.

"He stuck with me despite that though, and now he's the reason my family and I have stable living and don't have to worry about a source of food." Shane's father gave Alex some time to respond, but again he didn't. "Anyway, like I said, I don't think you're at any risk of losing any of them. They may be a bit scared of you, but that's natural. You and I both were when we found out werewolves weren't just a fable."

"Yeah," Alex said after another exhale.

"Alright, I have to go," Shane's father said as he slid his chair back and stood up. "My wife's waiting for me, and likely Shane too."

"Thanks, then. For coming," Alex said in reply.

"You're welcome." As his chair was slid back under the table, Shane's father stopped himself. "Oh, I just realized. I never introduced myself."

Alex glanced aside as Shane's father chuckled. He hadn't noticed up to now either.

"It's Michael, and our family name is Bryant. I'll introduce you to my wife when you come on the full moon."

Shane and Michael Bryant... "Alright." When Alex noticed Michael's hand held out, he reached over to grab and shake it. The strength he'd felt before was still there, but now he was less nervous about the act.

Chapter 27 - New Plans...

Sunday, Nov. 5th, 2011
Moon Phase - Waxing Gibbous
Time until the Shift - 4 Days, 12 Hours

After Shane's father left, Alex waited a few minutes before following suit. He could already see Shane asking what his father was doing meeting him, if any scents or something else gave it away, leaving him to hope Michael would keep what was asked of him to himself.

Just before noon the following day, while he was jumping between texting Nathan and Catherine, he saw a prompt appear with a text from Michael and switched over to it.

Michael B.: Alex, I forgot to tell you.
Since you'll be with us until you change back,
you'll need a change of clothes and some kind
of time-passer.

A text from Nathan came in while Alex typed a response. He didn't finish it before the second part came in.

Michael B.: You can bring them to the house, or
Shane can pick them up. Whichever works for you.

Alex soon decided on the latter before getting to work, putting aside what he would need. When 2:00 p.m. came on Sunday, he left the house with Bailey in tow, leading him to the area where he was supposed to hand the stuff over to Shane.

The local park was more crowded than he expected, and the east-bound breezes left him glancing around for a sign of Shane. As it happened, he arrived via the same creek route Alex had used his first night as a werewolf.

The sight of Shane got Bailey's tail to wag, even after Alex made him sit and stay. Privately, Alex hoped Shane's scent wouldn't unnerve Bailey.

What did happen was his dog stopped wagging his tail after trying to sniff at Shane, but didn't make any noise. "You're okay, boy," Shane told him, to which Alex shuddered a bit. "You got them?" Shane then asked.

Alex glanced around for a moment.

"You're not dealing drugs. Stop being so paranoid."

"Yeah, yeah," Alex replied before slipping his backpack off and unzipping the back pocket. He'd stuffed his clothing and a few books and comics into a thin trash bag, which Shane waited for him to hand over. "Nothing special in there, but if you mark them, I'll know."

Shane gave Alex a scowl at that remark.

"Speaking of marking," he said after a second, "what's going on with your friends?"

Alex took a moment to think of an answer. "They're fine."

"You sure about that?" Shane continued when Alex stalled. "You remember me saying they'll try not to act scared of you?"

Alex nodded.

"Don't let them drift away from you. If that happens, what reason would they have to safeguard what they know about you?"

Although Alex's thoughts immediately went to Catherine, he responded with, "That sounds a bit controlling."

"If they weren't your friends, sure."

"I'll see what I can do then."

"Good. You've still got a few days. Put them to use."

Shane departed before Alex could respond, though during the walk home, Shane's words eventually pushed him into texting Marcus, and asking if another get-together might be possible.

Before the day was through, a date and time had been decided upon.

Thursday, Nov. 9th, 2011
Moon Phase - Waxing Gibbous
Time until the Shift - 8 Hours

In the lead-up to Thursday evening, Alex was left dreading the moment when he would have to reveal his choice of meat supplier. While his friends didn't prod him for an answer, he stayed ready for the question if they meant to ask him.

As late afternoon came, he headed for Catherine's place of work to meet up with her and Marcus. The store was mostly empty when he arrived, though after catching Marcus's scent, he found both of them within the Sci-Fi section.

Catherine was already looking his direction when he rounded the corner and greeted them. "Anything good come in?" Alex asked, hoping to break any poor mood set between them.

"Yeah," Catherine began. "We got some good ones, I think."

"Already found a few DOOM novels," Marcus said, showing off two in his hands.

"Those aren't bad, strangely enough." Alex said before digging through the book pile himself. His friends stayed silent after that, but having not heard anything strange in their tones, he let them be until Nathan arrived.

"Still got half-an-hour, then I'm done," Catherine eventually said. Alex stuck around the Fantasy shelves after that, while Nathan headed for the nearby Mystery shelves, and Marcus the gaming section. Nothing but footsteps, intercom announcements, and light music sounded for the half-hour length, but once all four of them were outside and Catherine's uniform was replaced with a T-shirt, things slowly went back to feeling like this was a normal meet-up.

At a nearby sub shop, Alex tried to get more absorbed in the scents of the place, and to ease his concerns over what his friends were thinking—something that proved difficult as the chatter between the four of them seemed to wane once their orders were placed.

Marcus already asked... If he hasn't told Catherine...but why wouldn't he? When Alex's attention was pulled towards the rising moon outside, he stared at it for a time, then sighed quietly to himself.

"So," Marcus began after what felt like minutes of silence, "what's the plan this time?"

Alex glanced at him, then noticed the interest in Nathan and Catherine's expressions. "I'm not hunting any loose animals," he soon said.

"You found a meat supplier?" Catherine asked.

The hint of pleasure in her voice made Alex question his next words briefly. "Yeah. There was a company in Houston I had my eye on...but Shane's family made a better offer, so I'm going with them."

"For how long?"

"As long as it takes for things to die down, or me to find a supplier like theirs."

"'Things to die down?' How long could that take?" Marcus asked.

"Months, I'm sure."

"Well, at least they're willing to help you out," Nathan said.

"Yeah. I think they're doing it to keep themselves safe too, though," Alex replied. "If animals keep dying, the police will keep looking, and if those canines catch the scent of us…"

"Have you seen them doing that?"

"Once, when I confronted Shane last month."

"They weren't scared? Of him or you?" Marcus asked.

Alex shook his head, though now he wished such a reaction had occurred. "Unnerved, at best. They're too well-trained to be scared, at least I think." When his friends kept quiet, Alex continued. "Won't matter this time, though. Dad's giving me a lift to their place Saturday morning."

Nathan's response, one which Alex could almost anticipate, came first after some more seconds of quiet. "In the paddy-wagon, I suppose?"

Alex let a tiny smirk appear. "Yep."

"That'll be weird."

"Yeah, but I'll take it. Safer than sneaking though the neighborhood, even in the dead of night."

Catherine noticeably exhaled after that, as though she was letting some tension out. "Glad to know you're not doing anything crazy," she said.

"It was more Dad's idea than mine, to be honest. Shane wanted to escort me to his house originally, at three in the morning."

"You think that would've been safe?"

"More or less. There's barely anyone driving around that early in the morning, and the police wouldn't have the canine units at the ready."

"Regardless, I think your dad had the right idea."

"Same here," Marcus said. "No sense in taking risks at this point."

Alex tucked away the question he thought to ask in response.

"You want me to text you every so often again?" Nathan asked.

"If you want to. It'll be mid-afternoon when I change back, though."

"Then, Marcus, Catherine, can you both help me with that? Just send a text every few hours or so?"

The sight of his friends nodding at the request stuffed a lump into Alex's throat. As much as he wanted to tell them he'd be fine, that it wasn't necessary, for what it was worth, he'd take the support for however long he needed to be at Shane's house.

Chapter 28 - ...Old Routines...

Thursday, Nov. 9th, 2011
Moon Phase - Waxing Gibbous
Time until the Shift - 7 Hours

Back at home, Bailey was the first to greet him, though his excited attitude vanished after catching a scent from him. *You'll be alright, boy.* Alex thought as he kneeled then reached for his dog's head. Bailey's muzzle and nose followed his arm until it touched his fur. After a few strokes, he could tell his dog wasn't happy and stopped.

When his parents noticed him from their seats in the dining area, his mother was the first to comment. "How did it go?"

"Much better than last time," Alex replied.

"That's good to hear."

Alex nodded in response. As he headed towards the kitchen and closer to his mother, he noticed her reach for and grab his arm, stopping him on the spot.

"I'll be alright," Alex said, to which his mother stood up and embraced him, tighter than usual. Returning the gesture until he was let go, his father then approached and did the same.

Friday, Nov. 10th, 2011
Moon Phase - Full
Time until the Shift - Up

Alex woke from sleep to the feeling of his heart racing. He noticed the taste of blood in his mouth and the sharpness of his fangs a split-second later. When he placed a hand over his chest, he could feel his claws and developing pads through his T-shirt.

After a glance at the bloodstains on his pillowcase, he slipped out of bed and stripped free of his clothes. Bailey was nowhere in the room, but once he found him in the guest room, Alex's deepening breaths woke him.

Sorry, boy. Alex made for the kitchen next, grabbing the water he'd readied from the fridge. His muscles had grown halfway to their fullest already, and the entirety of the glass of cold water served as a perfect counter to his rising body heat.

What he knew was coming next pushed Alex to grab a dish towel and slip into the pantry. Once he was on his hands and knees, he held the towel near his mouth. When he felt the tension shoot through his calves, he gritted his teeth and blocked his mouth, the cloth blocking most of his reaction grunts and growls.

Then came the first strands of his pelt. Alex stayed on his knees, his paws following up the itching from the fur growth with comforting rubs.

With the second jolt down his spine, signaling the growth of his tail and ears, Alex lowered himself onto his back. Just his bones were left. He closed his eyes, curled his legs, and held the towel close.

When he heard the cracking of his jaw and skull, he gripped the cloth harder. As before, the first bones to change were in his legs, the stretching of his flesh, muscles, and bones sparking noises backed by unease. Then came his chest, which put a temporary end to his gasps, and then his face and jaw. The slackening of his bones was no easier than last time, but he was quicker to get his breathing under control when his bones settled into their new shapes.

Refreshed from sleep, yet suddenly sore in places thanks to the shift, Alex relaxed his tensed-up form and lay silent, past the point when his stomach began to growl. After another glass of water and several warm hot dogs, he returned to his room and lay back down until he felt truly ready to get up.

His parents roused a few hours later as he sat absorbed in one of his books. How huge his paws were, coupled with his claws, had made certain ones difficult to keep open, and free of accidental tears and punctures. By then also, despite his undrawn blinds, he had noticed several flashes of light outside. None were accompanied by thunder until it was close to daybreak.

The rain he was anticipating came suddenly hours later, while he was lounging around inside the garage. As the patter of water on the roof, concrete, and grass masked most of the sounds nearby, Alex let his olfactory sense catch the new scents the rain was bringing with it. Many of them were, as best as he could tell, bacterial in nature, coupled with hints of plant matter, all of which were drowning out scents he'd been picking up since going outside.

A smirk then spread across his muzzle when he imagined Shane showing up in the yard, looking like he'd just been hosed down for a bath, growling at the raindrops pelting him on the nose and ears. The chuckle that eventually got away from him came out as a scratchy bark, surprising him for a moment.

So that's what laughing as a werewolf sounds like, Alex thought as he went back to watching the rain.

As soon as the torrent slowed, he slipped back inside and after a snack, got back to reading. *Wonder if this is what Shane and his old man do every time this happens.* Remembering Michael's words about the thirty-six hours becoming a routine, he could see why he'd mentioned bringing something to help pass the time.

When he heard his phone sound the IM tone a short time later, Alex gave it a second, then picked it up when no more sounds came.

Catherine W.: Everything okay?

Alex smiled as he typed out his reply; Catherine had used the old chatroom with Marcus and Nathan included as receivers.

> *Alex S.:* Yeah. The house feels like a
> cage, though.

Catherine W.: Can't quite relate, but sorry
to hear that.

I'll get used to it, at some point, Alex thought as he put his phone aside. The next thought through his head was a daydream of being alone in a large, wooded area, one that, although the sun was lighting it up through overcast skies, felt completely safe. The idea was difficult to wipe free of his thoughts, even after some time gaming and an unsuccessful attempt at getting Bailey to come to him.

As his sense of cabin fever grew, Alex set his phone to autoplay some videos he liked before opening his bedroom window and lying back on his bed. With his eyes closed and his muzzle pointing up, the outside scents were quick to reach him, but offered only a slight dulling of the uneasy feeling.

Sheesh, only six hours... He let several videos play before reopening his eyes. By then the rain had returned, and more intensely than before. A check of his phone's weather app showed it was likely to stick around for a few days.

When Marcus texted him a short while later, he did so with a comment related to the statement to Catherine. Alex replied within a minute.

> *Alex S.:* Staying outside does help.
> Guess it'll be the garage for me for a while.

Marcus A.: What about tomorrow?

> *Alex S.:* I'll change back around 2:00 p.m.
> This won't be an issue after that.

* * *

As the time neared noon, Alex heard his father's truck coming up the driveway and slipped back inside. Resisting the urge to shake himself free of water, he waited near the entryway for his father to come inside; Bailey was quick to shower him with affection once he did.

"Did Shane or his dad contact you at all?"

Alex shook his head.

"So then, are you sure you just want me to drop you off?"

"Yeah. Shane will let me in." When his father didn't follow up, Alex added more. "By the way, I told the guys to text you if I don't respond to some texts they'll send me."

"Why? I thought you trusted this kid and his family."

"Just being safe."

Within the next half-hour, Alex's access to his parent's room, and the less visible door to the backyard, was cut off. His father was asleep shortly after, leaving him to pass the time as best he could until his mother came home. With ordered in pizzas set for dinner that night, Alex found his chance to hug both his parents and reassure them that he'd be fine.

Saturday, Nov. 11th, 2011
Moon Phase - Full
Time Until Human Again - 13 Hours

Alex awoke well before one the next morning. The rain from the previous day was still coming down when he did, though the thunder and lightning was mostly gone, and the hunger had yet to show, letting him snack on a few things before he found a spot near the front door windows to watch for his father.

As he did, a text came though from Michael.

Michael B.: On your way?

Alex S.: Not yet. Still waiting.

Michael B.: Shane's watching the street. One car just drove by, and I think parked nearby.

The twinge to his nerves Alex felt didn't last beyond a second.

Alex S.: Dad and I will be quick.

Michael B.: Keep us posted, then.

* * *

When his father at last arrived, Alex gripped his phone and keys tightly. Would his unease from before be stronger in this form? He shook his head and tried to downplay the idea before saying a quiet goodbye to his mother and slipping outside.

His unease perked immediately when he started to climb into the back of the cruiser. *Relax. Nothing's happening.* The radio chatter and numerous scents, ranging from vile to strange, gave him something to focus on as his father shut him inside and then continued driving. *This does feel weird.*

The drive lasted only a few minutes, though Alex stayed ready to duck in case another cruiser pulled up near his father's. When they stopped, he pulled his head up and looked around. There were numerous cars on the street and in the driveways, but no one in sight.

"Ready?" his father asked for a moment.

"Yeah. Open the door when you're ready."

His father waited for almost a minute before getting out and opening the door. Alex slid out once it did, crouching and swinging his head left and right as soon as he touched the ground. Seeing no one again, he bolted for the door, turning around and flashing a thumbs-up to his father as he got back inside his cruiser and drove off.

Chapter 29 ‑ ...And A New Approach

Saturday, Nov. 11th, 2011
Moon Phase - Full
Time until Human Again - 12 Hours

The scents the front door had held back were sucked outside as soon as Shane opened it. Alex found both Shane and Michael's scents immediately, prompting his pulse to climb and his will to move to fail.

"C'mon, get in here." Shane whispered, to which Alex looked around again before obeying. More scents were processed as the door shut behind him---none that reinforced his nerves, but plenty that proved how lived-in the house was, and that someone was cooking. "Dad's in the kitchen, if you skipped breakfast."

Alex waited for Shane to walk away before standing up again. The scents were making him hungry again, though part of him suspected it was the other hunger surfacing. After a minute, the scents won him over and he stepped lightly into the kitchen through the dining room.

What he found was Michael, in his seemingly eight-foot-tall werewolf form, crouched over the stove and cooking two packages of pork sausages. Despite the scene, when his head turned, Alex inched back some and his head dropped.

"You're fine, Alex. C'mon in," Michael said in a half-whisper. Though his words were welcoming, his voice was brimming with growls and Alex suppressed a swallow. Two links were all he took. "My friend should be here around six. As soon as he drops the meat off, you'll have your share."

"Thanks," Alex said before he nibbled the end off one of the links.

"When you're done, your stuff is in the room. Just keep quiet until my wife wakes up."

Alex only nodded.

"One last thing: keep some water with you. It'll help distract you if the hunger lasts beyond a few hours."

Alex nodded again, to which Michael handed him an oversized cup already filled with water and ice, and a few straws.

* * *

When the real hunger emerged, Alex took a breath to calm himself. *Just gotta wait it out.* As he did so, the cabin fever feelings returned, and intensified faster. Staring outside was no help, and he didn't want to open the window, despite no hint of alarm triggers.

Alex then went for his water. A few sips cooled his skin and chest but did little else.

When he heard a pair of light taps on the room's door a few minutes later, he was barely on his feet before the door swung open to reveal Shane. He slipped inside and swung the door shut behind him, though not all the way.

"Dad wants to know if you want to come outside while we wait for the delivery," he said in a similar growl-laced whisper.

Alex answered in short order. "How big is your garage?"

"About as large as yours."

"If that's what you're using, that's good enough for me."

Instead of replying, Shane simply gestured for Alex to follow. As he did, he walked through a patch of scents with hints of Michael's wife and felt his stomach relax, reminding him of what happened with his mother and her scent. Did Michael already trust him that much?

Once outside, Alex tucked the question away. Shane had been more on his case than his father from minute one, though now he couldn't help feeling some sympathy for them.

As the patter of rain continued around them, Alex followed Shane into the garage. Aside from a table with stools, one of which Michael was using, very little felt out-of-place. With Michael's form illuminated though, Alex could see the color similarities in his and Shane's pelts; his was an even split of black and tan, one almost German shepherd-like in pattern.

"You can leave the side door open," Michael said after Alex looked behind himself.

"I suppose this is where the meat stays?" Alex asked after he pulled out a stool to use.

"Oh, no, we eat inside. The kitchen's easier to clean up."

Alex nodded in response before glancing over at Shane, who was already fixated on the book in his paws. The comics he brought were burned through within minutes, leaving his phone and the one paperback he'd brought.

* * *

His father became the first person to text him close to an hour later.

Dad: How are things going?

Though Shane and Michael gave only a glance at the sound of the IM tone, Alex told them who it was, and what was said, before typing out his reply.

Alex S.: Fine. Just reading something and waiting for the meat delivery.

Dad: How long will that take?

Alex S.: An hour or two, I think.

Alex received no reply but was certain his father was satisfied.

A while later, another phone rang: Michael's. Shane's attention was ripped from the book in his paws at the ring tone, while Alex gave him and Michael only a glance. At least until he could tell the phone was being answered in speaker mode.

"Hello?" Michael began in as human a voice as he could muster.

"Mr. Bryant?" The voice was female.

"Yes."

"This is Houston EMS. Do you know someone named Yamato Ishida?"

Alex's pulse picked up at that sentence, and when he looked at Michael, it was as if he could feel the color draining from his face.

"Yes, he's a friend."

"Then, I'm sorry to tell you, he was involved in an accident within the last half-hour."

When Michael's eyes widened, and his muzzle inched open at the news, Alex knew. That was their meat supplier.

"He was breathing and responsive when we got him to the emergency room, but I don't know how badly he's hurt."

Michael had to force himself to respond within five seconds, but his voice was already slipping. "Which side was hit?"

"Driver's side, at the rear. His vehicle was totaled. Same with the one that hit him."

Michael's paws clenched as he tried to relax his breathing, and get his voice reigned in. "I see."

"I'll pass along your number to the staff. They'll call you if anything changes."

"Thank you." Michael didn't wait for the other line to hang up before stopping the call. As soon as he did, and his paws were placed over his eyes, Alex could hear his demeanor slipping, even though he said nothing out loud.

It was the sight of Shane coming up to and hugging his father that got Alex to turn away, and work to keep himself from seeming anything besides sympathetic. *Damn it. Now what?* All he could see happening was the three of them searching out an animal and having their fills before the sun rose, all in less than two hours, three at a stretch.

Despite the assumption, Alex did not speak. Shane and his father had to have been in this situation before; they would know how best to tackle it.

After what felt like several minutes, Michael's demeanor had recovered enough to let him speak without sounding too upset. "Alex, Shane, this is what we'll have to do. We need to decide on a place outside of town where we can get a large enough animal to feed the three of us."

Outside of town? Like where?

"I do know a few places with cattle and such, but whichever we choose, we have to do this quickly and save as much of the animal as we can."

With that, Alex was quick to picture Michael's wife driving them somewhere, letting them out, and then coming back for them when the time was right. What else that would entail, he could only speculate.

"Whichever place has the easiest animals to grab," Shane said after only a moment.

"If that place has sparse lighting, I'll agree," Alex said.

"Alright. I'll go wake Carol up. You two stay out here until I come back." It took Michael a minute to leave, though how tall he stood ensured Alex's attention never left him.

Shane made no remarks after his father left; Alex didn't feel like getting him to talk, and stayed quiet himself. The longer Michael stayed gone however, the easier it became to fixate on the growing hunger plaguing his stomach. Both Shane and Michael's scents had turned from concerning to repulsive with the onset of the hunger, which he minded much less than the alternative, and did his best to go along with.

When Michael returned, Carol wasn't with him. Instead, Alex heard her start the engine of the SUV he'd seen in the driveway, and inch backwards towards the garage door. Michael then directed both Shane and Alex to be ready, and to help him load a rolled-up tarp. As soon as the garage door came up and the rear of the SUV opened, the tarp was loaded, and Michael directed Shane and Alex into the back. He took the back seats once everything had been closed behind them.

By then Alex was once again noticing Carol's scent, and the tightening of his stomach relaxed again.

"Alright, Hon. Whenever you're ready," Michael said once he was inside.

"Where are we going?" Alex asked once he felt the SUV leave the driveway.

"It's a place west of here," Michael replied. "Close to Katy."

Alex didn't reply, and Shane kept quiet also.

"When we get there, if it's still raining, we'll decide on an animal before we leave the car. No one should be nearby, so noise won't be an issue, but we have to save what we can in case Yamato stays hospitalized for a while. The rest we can discard." Michael paused for a moment. "Alex?"

"Yeah?"

"I'm sorry your first time with us had to go this way."

Alex sighed quietly before he replied, and noticed Shane glance at him. "It's fine. So long as this hunger is dealt with."

It was a few minutes later when Alex realized he'd left his phone in the garage. A spike of cold tore through him and his pulse climbed as he thought of what would happen if his dad or one of his friends texted him and he was unable to reply.

Son of a bitch. Why did I forget that thing?

Shane noticed his change in demeanor, and increase in heartbeat, within a second. "What's wrong?"

Damn it... None of them should be up before six. "Nothing."

"Freaking out already?"

"Shane." Michael didn't need to say more to make things quiet again. "Alex, if you're worried about any of this, just lie back and breathe easy. Don't fixate on what's coming. You'll just stress yourself."

Alex took a moment before exhaling loud enough to give the impression that he was trying. By the time he felt the SUV slow down and move to drive over rougher terrain, his concerns had shifted towards his parents instead of his friends. If his father had texted him in the time since they'd left...

"We're almost there," Michael said.

Alex swallowed at that sentence. By that point, his hunger had built to where Carol's scent was drawing his attention more than the repulsive ones from Michael and Shane. The sooner that was gone, the better, and with the rain making less noise against the roof, Alex grew anxious to get out of the vehicle, more so when he began to ask himself if Michael and Shane were feeling the same way he was.

When the vehicle finally stopped moving, Alex heard the parking brake being set, and then the headlights switching off. Michael then shuffled his position to peer out of the nearest window, speaking up after the rain seemed to end. "I don't see anyone. Let's get out and go closer."

Shane wasted no time opening the rear door, though only a crack at first. The scents from outside washed over the ones inside the vehicle cabin as Alex waited for Shane to move. He found ones from horses, pigs, and at least two kinds of cattle, along with the other kinds of scents such a location housed, some urging a covering of his nose.

Once Michael had left the cabin, Shane followed suit. Alex then followed, but slowly, his attention shifting from thing to thing as he let himself down onto the soggy, stone-strewn ground. They'd driven quite a distance from the nearest road, but the still-existent lightning was randomly lighting the area up and playing havoc with his nightvision when it flashed.

The next rumble of thunder was when Michael spoke up, telling Alex and Shane to follow him. As he did, Alex let his attention focus on Shane. Unless Michael did all the work, which Alex doubted would be the case, Shane would be getting a part of his wish.

Otherwise, the winds were in their favor, and so was the seemingly empty area. The animals would be more focused on the weather, and what noise they would make wouldn't reach anyone of note.

As they drew closer to the stable, Michael led Alex and Shane in the direction of towering oak tree, coming half out of his all fours stance to look around again. "No one still," Michael said as he lowered himself back down. He then turned to face Alex and Shane. "I can see at least nine animals from here, but there's a lot more in there." Alex swallowed and licked his muzzle before Michael continued. "Remember, nothing too big, and Alex?"

"Yeah?"

"Before we do this, I want you to keep in mind: when you make your move, at any time when you must do this, go for the throat as quickly as you can, and do not let go until you know you're winning and your prey is giving out. It's hard to do, and I understand it's gruesome, but if you hesitate, you could wind up chasing a wounded animal, and they will either tire you out doing everything they can to keep away from you or fight you off. Do you understand?"

Alex nodded.

"Are you nervous about this?"

Alex nodded again.

"Do you think you could do it if I let you choose the animal?"

This time, Alex took a few seconds. The biggest he'd taken out was the doe, something much lighter than him. "I don't know," he eventually said.

"Then, how about the alternative I mentioned to you before?"

Alternative? It took a second longer for Alex to remember what that was. "Probably."

This time, Michael nodded. "Then I have an idea. You two, wait here." When Michael returned, he was walking on three paws, the fourth holding a leather holster and the pistol sheathed within it.

It was a .44 chambered revolver, with a trigger guard barely wide enough to let one of Michael's digits slip into place. The rounds were all hollow points, which Alex knew would tear through flesh with little issue.

After the cylinder was locked back in place, Michael sheathed the weapon. "Here's what I think we should do. We all decide on the animal, then you, Alex, take a shot at it. Shane and I will then go after it, if it survives the shot." Michael then turned to Shane. "Are you fine with that, Son?"

"So long as he doesn't point that thing at me," Shane said, his attention not wavering from the revolver.

"I know how to use these things," Alex responded.

"Then, is this something you're willing to do?" Michael asked.

Alex stared at the revolver for a moment, then nodded.

"Alright then," Michael said. "Let's go."

The animal the three of them decided upon was one of three older calves. Despite the unnerved noises the animals began to make at the presence of the three werewolves, the calves stayed asleep, or so it seemed to Alex.

His pulse remained elevated as he unsheathed the revolver, cocked the hammer, and steadied his aim, his index claw set in the gap between the trigger and guard. His emotions picked up slight strength in turn.

For what felt like minutes, Alex didn't fire. He kept watch on the flashes of lightning through the corner of his eye. One moment was what he was waiting for, and thankfully Shane and Michael were keeping silent.

It took some time, but when it--a loud, cracking boom of thunder--came, Alex's claw and digit depressed the revolver's trigger. The gunshot stood out very little in turn, and the calf lay dead after only a few twitches.

The animals around them reacted in terror at both loud noises; Shane and Michael gave Alex only quick congratulations before reminding him that time was of the essence. With that, he sheathed the revolver. The deed was done.

All that was left was to feed.

Shane and Michael were first to enter the pen after Alex's successful kill. Shane kept behind his father and watched as he examined the carcass. Michael then looked back toward Alex.

"You killed it, so the first piece is yours," he said.

Alex glanced at Shane in turn. No disappointment or similar emotions showed on his face. His father had the last word, and he knew it.

Michael took the revolver and leather sheath from Alex as he came closer, then let him get into position. At first he was unnerved at the sight and felt his pulse rise, but when the smell of blood reached his muzzle, his stomach reopened.

His first piece was taken from the calf's front left limb, a small piece that he finished within a few bites. By then, Michael had set the revolver aside and gone for the calf's ribs. Shane went last, continuing the work his father had begun.

Alex lost track of time as the three of them ate their fills. To his relief, Michael and Shane didn't seem willing to feed near the calf's abdomen, though at one point, Shane attempted to grab another piece before his father was finished. The deep, rumbling growls that Michael sounded toward his son, and the sight of Shane's ears folding back before his body inched back, sent a quiver through Alex's body, and he pulled his next piece before Shane did.

When Michael spoke again after who knew how long, Alex reacted like his voice was meant to jump-scare him. "You both full?"

Shane took another piece in answer. Alex eyed the carcass briefly before nodding.

"Are you sure?"

Alex nodded again, now with his attention on the blood and flesh staining Michael's muzzle and teeth.

"Be certain. Take a few bites more." Michael then looked toward Shane, who only eyed him in response. "I'll be right back." The pen's door was then inched open, and with the revolver held in one paw, Michael left them.

"You heard him," Shane said.

"I know," Alex said. The spot he had been feeding from was stripped close to the bone, as were the spots Shane and Michael had chosen. Taking more from further up the limb was what he chose.

When Michael returned, he looked over the carcass for a moment, then spoke. "Alex, give Shane a hand with this. I'll lift from the back legs." Shane then went for the calf's head, leaving Alex to lift by its back and shoulders.

Despite the three of them contributing, the weight of the calf's carcass meant a slow walk back to the SUV, the still-pouring rain soaking into their pelts as they went. The droplets caused a few twitches of muzzles when they landed.

"So," Alex began as they prepared to lower the carcass onto the tarp Michael prepared, "what happens now?"

"Let's get in the car first," Michael said as they all finally let go, the SUV's rear dipping an inch from the weight of the carcass. "You're in the back." He and Shane wasted no time closing the rear door once Alex was in, and seconds later, they joined him.

Carol then started the SUV, and once moving again, Michael continued. "As soon as we get back, we'll carve off what we can and go from there."

"What about the rest? The bones and all that?"

"No need to worry about that. I'll deal with it."

Shane didn't add anything to his father's words, leaving Alex to wonder what they used to do in situations like this, as well as find ways to avoid staring at the carcass lying next to him.

Eventually they began taking turns and following roads he recognized, and it wasn't long before the SUV began backing up into a driveway. Despite seeing no hints of police cruisers, Alex still felt a touch of concern. He'd already thought up a number of answers to whatever his father would ask him---and if his friends had texted him, he had them covered as well---but the SUV had been parked outside when they arrived. If his father had driven by and noticed that it was missing...

As the SUV came to a stop near the garage, Alex did his best to keep calm. Keeping his attention away from where he knew his phone was, Shane and Michael were soon helping him lift the carcass out of the car and into the garage. The table they had used earlier in the night, once the tarp was laid down, became the spot where their kill was displayed.

Once Michael and Shane began looking for the tools they needed, Alex snatched his phone and noticed a light blinking near the screen. Despite the blood still caking his paws, he turned his phone on. He'd missed three texts, and a phone call. One each from his father, and the other texts from Marcus and Nathan. All of them had come through minutes after the trip to the ranch had begun.

When he glanced at Shane and Michael again, neither of them were paying attention to him. Hoping it would stay that way, Alex returned his attention to his phone. They could do without him for a few minutes anyway.

Epilogue - Years Later and Back In The Day

Friday, April 3rd, 2015
Moon Phase - Waxing Gibbous
Time until the Shift - 3 Hours, 10 Minutes

"Need another drink, boy?" Alex asked as he and Bailey neared a street corner. Bailey only looked back at him. "Alright. Let's go." They then turned down Rozelle Avenue and within a minute, stopped again.

525. The only house on the whole street with a "For Lease" sign in the yard. The grass had recently been cut, yet after almost two months, there was still no hint of a renter.

Within a few seconds of looking over the house, Alex took a breath to shake off the pressure surfacing in his throat. He then led Bailey up the driveway of the house, toward the backyard and garage.

As he did, the time he'd spent in the house started to cycle in and out of his thoughts. The many hours he'd spent waiting for meat, and the rarer instances of simply being there to talk to Shane or his friends and family. He'd warmed up to them over time, and in the end, how he'd felt at the news that they were planning to move simply refused to leave the depths of his mind.

Still, they had earned the house they'd bought, a quiet little spot north of Houston near Spring with a lot of wooded land nearby. Though he was happy for them, becoming the only werewolf for tens of miles was more unpleasant than he expected.

When Alex heard Bailey make a curious grunt, he looked down to find his pet wagging his tail and staring up at him. "I know, boy," he said after gathering his composure and before reaching down to pet his dog. "Thanks."

As they walked away from the house, Alex heard his phone sound an IM tone. Nathan had climbed to the top of his messaging list with a question about how he was doing. Shane, Michael, Marcus, and Catherine were in order below him.

* * *

Monday, October 1st, 2001
Moon Phase - Full
Time until Human Again - 27 Hours, 9 Minutes

It started with a dark forest and ended in clenching terror at being hunted. When Michael awoke, he felt as if he'd been sleeping under a quilt with chilled bones. His wife was lightly snoring next to him, to his relief.

His fatigue gone, yet his pulse raised thanks to what his brain had displayed, Michael closed his eyes and tried to forget the nightmare. It took some time, and by then he was feeling an urge to get up and wander the house, maybe fix himself something.

Getting off the bed without waking his wife was a slow process, though he eventually slipped out of the room into the hallway with barely a sound. With Shane's room to his left, he made a detour, finding the door open. His son's humanoid werewolf form was splayed chest-down atop his bed, as though he was an oversized puppy exhausted from a day of playing.

A smile spread across Michael's muzzle at the sight, though in the back of his mind he questioned when, or if, his son would ever change forms like he did. When it could happen, and if he would be ready for it, remained a personal concern as well. He'd never felt his bones crack, only heard it.

After checking the front door and deadbolt, if only to calm himself further, Michael made himself a glass of water and sat down in the kitchen. It was nearing two months since they'd moved in, and by now, the many scents within the walls, the carpet, and the rooms themselves were taking on a familiar edge. Hundreds of details about the previous residents had made themselves known since then, none he'd found suspect, but eventually the scents of his family would take their places and the house would feel that much more like home.

Bonus Short Story

Saturday, January 26th, 2013 - Erie, Kansas
Moon Phase - Full
9:07 p.m.

Smooth road for miles, then suddenly, hard bumping. No mistake about it. Flynn was finding a spot off-road to park. At one point, something he drove over threw me up high enough to bump the cover of his truck bed, then land back on the bed with a thump, my muzzle almost taking a frontal hit as well. Regardless of what Flynn had planned for me, I was anxious to get out and move around.

While attempting to brace myself against further ragdoll incidents, I began to smell things I knew were related to the Neosho River. He came to a stop a minute later, shut the engine off, and then got out without a word. At least until the bed's latch was down.

"All set out here, man," he said.

Already, I could see trees, shrubbery, and the settled snow on both, along with the unhindered glow of the full moon. After sliding out and looking around, it seemed we were just north of the river, likely along Pryor Road.

"There's nothing around here," I said before focusing on Flynn. He was wrapped up in a winter coat and hat; I was wearing a self-made pair of boots and my fur.

"It's not here," Flynn replied. "It's a bit of a walk to the south."

"Okay. What exactly is it, then?"

"You'll see."

He started moving soon after, and I followed after a moment. Though I found it odd that he wouldn't say what the thing was, I had the impression that it was important, or at least interesting. It had to be if he was getting me away from the house at this hour.

After ducking behind a clump of bushes to avoid a truck's headlights, we were past the road and followed the river east. It gradually curved south and, after a time, Flynn spoke up again. "That way. We're coming up on it." He then dimmed the flashlight he was holding.

"Expecting something?" I asked. I got no answer besides a gesture to keep quiet. Nothing stood out as I tried to see what Flynn was referring to. The north to south direction of the wind wasn't helping either. All the scents that the town of Erie was giving off were mixing with what the river was giving off.

Then after a few more minutes, I began to see what Flynn was leading me towards. It was nestled within one of the horseshoe loops of the river, hidden within a large clump of trees.

Someone built a house out here? Huh.

As we drew closer, it became clearer that this "house" was more a shell than anything. It wasn't makeshift, but it had been destroyed by some kind of fire. The flames had burned parts of the nearby trees, while the snow on and around the shell was a good indication the fire had started and ended days ago.

As we drew closer, I began to suspect Flynn had brought me out here to put my senses to their fullest use. No doubt all he could smell were hints of ash, if that.

When he came to a stop, we were close enough for me to catch hints of what this shell of a house was giving off. None of them warranted caution to my mind, and I saw nothing around to justify suddenly going quiet. The closest noises were the cars driving by on the other side of the river.

"What is it?" I asked.

"Just making sure," Flynn replied.

I waited a few seconds before continuing. "I take it you found something here before."

"Not really. Just seemed like the kind of place a werewolf would hide out or make their home."

"Huh. Well, I'll give this place a once-over. See if anything stands out."

As I began circling the building, Flynn turned his flashlight back on and circled in the opposite direction. At first, the scents from the structure were nothing of note. Charred wood and plaster, among other kinds of material. Very little had been spared from the flames, and the empty rooms I could see into showed few signs of leftover items, or any hint that something was using the place as a hideout.

I'd almost circled the structure when something rank reached my nose. It was weak, but it didn't belong there. Of that I was sure. Curious what was giving the scent off, I looked over the closest room first. Its size and wood flooring seemed in line with a master bedroom, but nothing else stood out. I then went down to all fours, hoping the scent would better reveal its origin.

After a short while I noticed it again, and after pushing past the charred walls, my pace slowed. The flooring was littered with debris, and the sight of a nail sticking through the snow only encouraged a slower pace. Knowing I couldn't avoid leaving impressions, I made a mental note to scrub any evidence of my presence before we left.

As I moved closer to the source, I could hear Flynn continuing his search. Nothing vocal yet, just footsteps.

After a little more time, the scent had built in strength to where I was confident that it was only a few yards from me. As it happened, the source was under a bit of snow.

It was a clump of bloodstained bandages, the blood itself dried up. I couldn't tell if it was human or werewolf, but the presence of such a thing, despite how innocuous it seemed, was enough to draw out an uneasy feeling.

"Flynn, over here," I said. It took just seconds for him to reach me. "Got some bloodstained stuff here."

He focused his flashlight beam on it as I pointed it out. "Human, or..."

I shrugged. "I don't know if werewolf blood smells different than human blood, so your guess is on par with mine." After pulling the find out of the snow, it turned out there was more than I thought on the wrappings. Too much for it to be from anything but a human or werewolf.

For a time, none of us said a word. Flynn, however, moved his flashlight around the area, likely to check for impressions that would confirm what was there.

"No sign of anything else," Flynn said.

"Fresh snowfall earlier today, don't forget," I replied.

"Oh, right."

"Still, this isn't that fresh. Maybe a day old at worst."

"It's something, though."

"Possibly." I then hung the wrapping on a nearby piece of wood. If I was going to cover my tracks, removing something like this before we left felt like a good idea as well. As Flynn began to walk away, something struck me, and I asked him to wait. "Just a second. Keep that flashlight on the snow."

Flynn did just that, and I started to dig. The fresh layer gave way to more compacted snow, under which I expected to find some hints of blood droplets or the like. Something to give me more of an idea why that bloodstained stuff was there.

It wasn't long before I found droplets soaked into a compacted layer of snow. The flooring underneath them was charred and wet, but I could just catch the scent of more soaked into the wood. Someone had been here while bleeding.

I then looked at Flynn, and nodded. "There's more."

"So, what should I do?" Flynn asked.

"Keep that flashlight on this area. I'll keep digging." Flynn did just that, and I soon dug away what remained of the snow. That was when I found a few ripped pieces of fabric. None of them were burned, just stiff from the snow and cold. Their black color had hidden them well.

"Ripped fabric and bloody bandages..." Flynn began.

"Odd find, that's for sure."

"Any scents on it?"

I held all the pieces near my nose and took a few sniffs. Nothing registered, and I shook my head. If these bits had held a scent, the snow had claimed it.

"Maybe something else will turn up in the rest of this snow?"

I hummed in response and looked over the area near me again. If blood had dripped onto compacted snow, then been snowed over...

This time, instead of digging straight to the deepest parts, I brushed away the nearest soft top layer of snow. Eventually, more droplets were found, as well as a spray pattern I couldn't identify, but along with them was a noticeable print hidden in the bottom layer. One similar in shape to my paws, with more blood in its recesses.

The sight caused my pulse to jump. As if Flynn could feel it, he said almost exactly what I was thinking. "So there was a werewolf here."

A glance was all I responded with. Now things were adding up, and I was growing curious about what else could be hidden nearby.

"Watch for nails if you're stepping around here." I told him.

"Think that would explain the blood and this other stuff?"

"No doubt. Get one of those in your hand, and that'll take a while to heal."

Flynn audibly winced at that. I then took back the bloodied fabric I found and gave it another sniff. Though I had my doubts I'd ever smell it or something like it again, getting an olfactory feel of it couldn't hurt.

Not long after, Flynn and I were searching the once-master bedroom side by side. The collapsed roof and walls had left hundreds of puncture hazards on the floor, which we threw aside as we found. We hunted for what felt like an hour yet found no hints of who this other werewolf was. Even the blood I had found only went so far out of the shell of a house.

To some extent, I expected that, but finding out there was another werewolf in the area was a start.

Was it the one that had attacked and bitten me, or another one? Were there more than one, all hiding somewhere around here? As vast as the plains and wooded areas around Erie were, for all I knew there were more than two.

"What time is it?" I asked once I felt we wouldn't find anything else.

"Ten forty-three."

I sighed, a cloud of white wafting from my muzzle. "At this point, I think we should call it a night and head back."

"You sure?"

"Yeah. If this one had left something else here, we'd have found it by now."

Flynn didn't immediately respond in favor of looking around. I could tell he wasn't convinced, and he eventually stood up. His first destination was a smaller room next to the master bedroom, then another next to that.

Then he held his flashlight on something for more than a few seconds. Curious what it was, I stood up and moved closer.

"What's that?" he asked when I came close enough. What I saw was what looked like a bit of puffy fabric poking up out of the snow. At first, nothing of note, but then how large the lump of snow under it looked made me think something was hidden there.

Being careful to avoid potential poking hazards, the fabric it turned out was the top handle of a backpack, untouched by flames yet buried in both compacted and fresh snow. Flynn kept the flashlight beam on it and me as I made my way back to him.

By then I had noticed several scents the snow had kept me from noticing; the top handle of the backpack, if not the pack itself, was lacking any real scents, as though they'd been scrubbed.

"What's in there?"

"Let's find out," I said after looking around to make sure we were alone.

The backpack seemed well-stuffed, and once it was opened, dozens more scents were let out for me to notice. Bodily and chemical ones were the first I noticed, a few registering familiarity. The things the pack contained were what one would expect from an overnight stay in a hotel: fresh clothing, hygiene products, and the like. Seeing all that, I didn't wait to start digging. I knew my own scents would mix with the ones in the pack, but if it contained what I hoped it would, that was a small price to pay.

Eventually, I felt it. A folded bundle of leather. As soon as I pulled it out, I wasted no time searching the wallet for some kind of ID. In the corner of my eye, I could tell Flynn was intrigued to see who the owner was.

The driver's license was stashed in another flap of the wallet. Kevin Millson was the name on it.

I didn't recognize the name or face, but Flynn did. Apparently, this Kevin worked for a shipping company, which mostly explained why I didn't recognize him. With that in mind, I took several whiffs of the scents the backpack had held, all the while, a flicker of disgust and anger began welling in my head.

I ended the scent-memorizing session with shoving the wallet back into the pack, hardly caring if things looked like they had before, and zipping every open pocket back up. Flynn kept quiet as I put the backpack back and covered it up with enough snow to hide everything but the handle as before.

"All set?"

"Almost." I replied after a second. "Could you turn around for a minute?"

Once Flynn did so, I crouched down and marked the snow near the pack with my scent. If this guy was the werewolf who had bitten me, leaving a clue that I knew who he was and where he lived, if not what he smelled like, felt like the perfect "I'm onto you".

Flynn and I then left the area after covering our tracks, the trek back to his truck letting the things I felt bleed out of me. Almost two years with no hard ideas, and now I had several.

"Thanks again for bringing me out here, man." I said after a while.

"My pleasure," Flynn replied, after which he grabbed and shook my paw.